RICH BOY MAF
DEMETTREA

D1508151

MAR 16

Rich Boy Mafia 2
By Demettrea

RICH BOY MAFIA 2
DEMETTREA

Acknowledgments and Dedications

This book is dedicated to my mom who is a cancer survivor.

First and foremost I want to thank my lord and savior, Jesus Christ. Without him nothing is possible. Thanks to my husband who has been rocking with me through it all. You pushed and promoted and I appreciate you for it all. This is only the beginning; the sky is the limit. To my kids, everything I do is for you. Thanks to my granny who's there for me no matter what. I am still a spoiled brat because of you. Thanks to my mommy for promoting my work and being there through it all.

My girls, my rounds, my sistahs, where do I start? You all have been there for me. We have laughed together, cried together and talked shit together. I couldn't have asked for a better set of friends. Forever my sisters, Gio, Cassie Lola (Bandz), Shay and Eb. I love y'all crazy asses.

To my loyal readers that stay in my inbox daily. You ladies are funny and you tell me the real. Erin McConnell, Tenita Thompson, Victoria Thomas, Shaniqua Morgan, Pookie Sumbler-Lewis, and Teba Bate.

RICH BOY MAFIA 2
DEMETTREA

To my Publishing family; Leo Sullivan, it is such an honor to work with someone so humble. I have been a reader of yours since Triple Crown and now to be a part of your team is great. Nika Michelle, Shelli Marie, Lola Bandz, Sunny Giovanni, Rio Terrell, Karmel Divine, Coco J, Teruka B, Destiny Henry, I hope I'm not forgetting anyone but if I am charge it to my head and not my heart.

My faves from PDP, Atiba, Aija (AMB), Yanni (The Baby), Luciana, Lucy, Tynessa, Janelle, and Jodacie. I am proud of each of you.

To my sisters Taylor and Raquel, I love you babies. Thanks to anyone that has read my work and told someone else about my work. You rock!

Thanks to my crazy co-workers for all the laughs during this process; Jade, Diamone, Raven and Jah'naye. And yes I'm writing y'all in my next book. (Lol)

If I forgot you it wasn't on purpose.

Chapter One

Everything Ain't Always What it Seems

As King sat in the dirty cell he thought about his actions. He didn't know whether he was sorry or not for beating Imran, but what he did know was that someone was playing games with his life. He had been locked up for two days now and had yet to contact anybody. He knew his brother Harlem would have something to say about his careless actions and he just wasn't trying to hear it. The way he felt, he'd never be in another relationship again. He felt as if love would be his downfall and he couldn't have that. He had too many people that looked up to him as the leader of RBM and he'd worked too hard to let his empire fall. His new attitude was "Fuck bitches, get money."

"Pierre! You're going home." King should have known Harlem would find out that he was locked up. King may have been the leader of RBM but Harlem was that nigga, and nothing went down without him knowing. He ran the streets of Detroit. Even in his retirement he had a say in what went down. He got up and waited for them to unlock the cell. King was led to the front desk where he waited to get his property back. That's when he saw Tish waiting. He did a double take because she was the last person that he expected to see.

"What the fuck you doing here?" He wasted no time with pleasantries. It was no secret that she was on his list of least favorite people.

"Well hello to you, too." She smiled but never answered his question.

Man, cut the bullshit. How did you even know I was here?" he tried a different approach with her. Something about her being here didn't sit too well with him.

"A little birdie told me you was here and I checked it out and figured you might have needed someone to bond you out. So here I am." King didn't buy her story but he decided to keep that to himself for now. He didn't know what was going on but he didn't trust anyone at the moment.

"Whatever." He walked out the police station and started up the street. He was looking for a cab when Tish pulled up beside him. She was trying any and everything to get back in good with King. She knew all about the issues with him and Ryan; mainly because she had something to do with them. He ignored her and flagged down a cab. He may not have been dealing with Ryan at the moment but he damn sure wasn't fucking with Tish's ass. He headed to the one place he knew he wouldn't have to deal with anyone: his mom's house.

~ ~ ~ ~

It had been two weeks since King had walked out on Ryan. She couldn't believe it had come to that. It seemed as if she wasn't meant to be happy. Everything that could go wrong did, but please believe she was willing to do whatever was needed to fix the situation. Ryan was about to show a side of her that no one had ever seen. She was ready to show the lengths that a real woman goes through to protect her family. Somebody had violated and needed to be dealt with, and she was going to be the one to handle it.

Ryan knew Mia was a gangster chick – that's why she was enlisting her help with the plans she had to get revenge. She was about to turn Imran's world upside down and he didn't even know it. When it was all said and done, King was coming home.

Ryan met Mia at Olive Garden for lunch and to run her plans by her. She didn't know if Mia was going to go for it or not but she was doing it with or without her help.

"Hey, lady!" She gave Mia a hug before sitting down.

"Hey, mama. I'm so glad you wanted to do lunch because between Harlem and the kids my ass is going crazy. I needed this break. Hell, we need to do it more often." Mia joked seriously.

"For sure, sis. Now I know we needed this lunch but I have something to run by you. I need your help. Keep in mind I'm doing this with or without your help, but I'd rather have your help." She raised her eyebrow at Ryan. For some reason Mia knew that some shit was about to go down, and being the friend she was, there was no way she'd let Ryan handle it alone.

"What the hell are you up to, Ry?" she asked as the waitress approached their table.

"Can I start you ladies off with something to drink?" The waitress was a blonde chick with a bunch of make-up and Botox. Mia was trying her hardest not to laugh in her face.

"I'll just have a coke," Mia replied as she looked over the menu.

"Same for me," Ryan ordered. She just needed her to go away so she could go over her plan with Mia.

"So what's this bright plan that you have mama?" Mia asked as she checked her phone.

"Well someone set me up. I have never slept with Imran. Did I think he was attractive? Hell yeah, but I never crossed that line with him. I met him in the mall a while back when King and I were having issues, but I didn't know they knew each other. Plus the video that King was watching was footage that was shot in our home. So what I need to find out is who the hell was in my house and who wants to destroy my relationship with King?' Mia's mouth was wide open.

"Let me ask you this; have you all heard from Tish?" That raised a red flag.

"Now that you mention it, that bitch did just up and disappear. But for some reason I feel Imran has a big part in this shit. I have to figure this mess out and quick, but have you seen King?" Ryan missed him and hadn't spoken to him since he walked out. The last two weeks had been pure hell without him.

"Wait, you haven't spoken to him?" Mia asked with a confused look on her face.

"Uh, no; that's why I asked you." Ryan looked at Mia for answers. She just wanted to know that King was okay.

"He's been staying at his mom's house. I thought you knew that," Mia responded as the waitress approached the table again.

"I'll have the chicken and shrimp Alfredo," Mia said as she looked over the menu.

"I'll have the same," Ryan quickly said. Food was the last thing on her mind but she wanted the waitress to leave.

"So has he said anything about coming home?" Ryan had hope in her heart that King would come home and they'd work things out. She had never felt for anyone the way she felt for him. He was her soul mate and she just couldn't fathom the idea of being with anyone else.

"Nah. He's been real quiet. You know, kind of to himself. He won't even talk to Harlem. I'm actually worried about him," Mia voiced. She was really close to King and was usually the one he went to for advice but that hadn't happened this time. It was as if he was in a state of depression and that was new to everyone. King had never been as close to a female as he was with Ryan.

"Damn, I feel responsible because I never should have spoken a word to Imran. But I swear we didn't do anything. He tried and I fought him off. Plus I feel like someone set me up because we don't have cameras in our house. I mean, unless King put them there to spy on me,"

12

Ryan stated, now thinking back to a conversation she had with King about some text messages.

"What the hell is this?" He passed her the phone.

She surveyed the message then looked at King as if she really didn't know what was up. "I'm assuming they have the wrong number."

"Yeah, okay. Let me find out."

"Ryan, did you hear me?" Mia asked, bringing her out of her thoughts.

"Huh? I'm sorry girl. I spaced out." Mia looked at Ryan with a raised brow. This mess between her and King was beginning to be a bit much and something had to be done.

"Look, Ma, I'm not one to judge; hell, Harlem and I have had our share of problems. But I will tell you this; if you love that man, then be patient. Let him deal with what he's dealing with and just be there for him. Especially when he goes to court." Mia loved Ryan like a sister and she knew in her heart that King would be back home eventually. He had to, because love trumped all.

"Thanks, Mia. I really appreciate it," Ryan said sincerely.

"Anytime. Now let's go shop." Mia paid the bill and they headed out.

~ ~ ~ ~

King had been away from his kids too long and he missed them. As much as he hated to admit it, he missed Ryan as well, but he wouldn't allow his barrier to fall. Whenever he would think of her it made him mad. He wanted to hate her but that was easier said than done.

King headed to the home that he once shared with Ryan. No matter what they were going through his kids would not suffer. He pulled up behind Ryan's car and killed the engine. He sat there thinking for a good ten minutes before he finally decided to get out and head to the door. His stomach was in knots. He didn't know how he would feel seeing Ryan again but he had to suck it up. He used his key to let himself in. It felt strange being there after being away for almost a whole month.

He heard the TV blaring from the family room so that's where he headed. Ryan was on the floor playing with Christian while Chasity was in her bouncer. He didn't see Cameron, which meant he was probably with

Mia. He decided after he left there he'd go by and grab him.

"Hey," King spoke. Ryan smiled and spoke back.

"Hey." He walked over to Chasity and picked her up.

"Where is Cam?" King asked, trying to make conversation.

"With Mia, as usual. You know I can never keep that boy home.

"Yeah, I know. I'll probably stop by and pick him up for a little bit." King was playing with Chasity and she was smiling because she recognized her dad. Ryan watched King with their daughter and she felt her heart swell. That was the man she loved with everything in her. Realizing King was avoiding looking at her, she decided to leave the room. She had never felt so uncomfortable. They were strangers to each other now. Ryan put Christian in his bouncer.

"I'm going to run their bath." Without waiting for a response from King she left the room. She was in a real emotional state. When Ryan made it to the bathroom she broke down. The tears that had been threatening to fall had finally been let lose. Every pent up emotion that

Ryan had held in for the past month was released at that moment. If she hadn't let go when she did Ryan would have been on her way to having a nervous breakdown. The things she had been through with past relationships and the things she was dealing with now had taken a toll on her. Ryan's heart broke in two because of the hurt she had caused King. It was never intentional and if she could she would definitely take it back.

King heard Ryan's cries and he felt some type of way. Yeah, he was still mad at her but he loved her. To see her hurting hurt him. He wanted to comfort her but didn't want to give her the wrong impression. He definitely was not trying to get back with her but she needed him at this moment. *Fuck it,* he thought as he put Chasity back in her bouncer.

King walked into the bathroom without knocking and pulled Ryan into his arms. He had a soft spot for her and would always be there for her. He just didn't think they'd be in a relationship; at least not now.

"It's okay, Ma. I'm here for you. We're gonna get through this." King rubbed Ryan's back and she felt safe in his arms, even if only for a minute.

"Thanks, King." Ryan moved from his embrace.

She appreciated him being there but she didn't want just some of him. She wanted all of him.

"You okay, Ma?" he asked, concerned.

"Yeah. I'm going to get the bath ready for them." Ryan busied herself running bath water for the twins. King didn't really know what else to say so he left. He couldn't even be around Ryan right now because he had mixed emotions about the whole situation. Until he figured some things out he would have to stay away.

Chapter Two

I Got Yo' Back, Boy

It was the day of King's court date. The day could bank on a lot of things. Ryan walked in the courtroom looking fly in her two-piece pinstripe suit. Her hair was pulled into a bun and her lips were popping with M.A.C. lip gloss. Everything about her screamed "bad bitch." She held her head up high and had confidence that King would be walking away today, especially if Imran didn't show up. And being that King was who he was she didn't have a doubt. King was that nigga.

Ryan was sitting down as King walked through the doors. Even though things weren't the best between them she still had his back. Harlem, RBM, and all their family walked in behind King. Helen sat next to Ryan and hugged her.

"Hey, mama," Ryan spoke. She still chilled with King's mom like nothing ever happened. Helen adored Ryan and hoped that her son got himself together.

"Hey, sweetie. Don't worry; he has one of the best lawyers," Helen assured Ryan. King looked back at his wife and mom sitting together and smiled. He and Ryan weren't on good terms but she was still here supporting him. That's why he married her; because she had his back. Ryan smiled back. That was a start. Before he wouldn't even look at her now she got a smile.

"All rise. The honorable Judge Gregory Hicks presiding." Everyone rose as the judge entered the courtroom. Ryan suddenly got butterflies in her stomach. They had reduced the charges to assault because Imran had recovered and refused to press charges. Ryan didn't know what but she knew Imran was plotting something and that she had to get him before he came for King. She felt it was her fault that he was in this position so she would always do what was needed to protect her King, whether they were together or not.

As the judge looked over the paperwork in front of him everyone became extremely quiet. No one knew what to expect because this judge had a reputation for being a hard ass.

"What evidence have you submitted, council?" The judge turned towards the prosecutor. The prosecutor was an older white man who was after King or anyone associated with RBM.

"Well, your honor, we had several witnesses that saw the defendant beat the victim with no remorse whatsoever."

"And where are these witnesses?" the judge asked.

"That's the thing your honor, no one is here today so I was going to ask for a recess to find out where they are." The judge looked at the prosecutor once more before speaking. You would have thought that as much as they wanted King they would have had their evidence together.

"So what you're telling me is you have wasted my time with this case. You have no evidence yet you've brought charges against this man."

"Your Honor—" The prosecutor began but was cut off by the judge.

"Case dismissed. Get out of my courtroom, counselor." King felt a huge burden lifted off of him. God had really been by his side. Ryan stood and proceeded towards the exit. The charges had been dropped and there was no need for her to stick around. Everyone was trying to congratulate King but he was trying to get to Ryan before she left. He was really thankful for her being by his side even though they were separated.

"Aye, thanks y'all, but I need to catch up with Ryan before she leaves." He didn't wait for anyone to respond. He needed to thank her. He caught her as she was getting in her car.

"Aye, Ryan," he called out and she turned around. He jogged over to her car.

"Hey, what's up, King?" King couldn't stop thinking of how cute she was. She was flawless even after having three kids.

"I wanted to thank you for being here for me, Ma. Despite everything we're going through you are still riding with a nigga and I appreciate that." Ryan smiled. It felt good to actually hold a conversation with King and not be fighting.

"You know I'm riding with you until the end. Even if we're not together." Ryan winked at him and got in her car. As she was pulling off she honked her horn. Ryan was a bad bitch and she knew it; and so did King.

******

"Cameron, go get your pajamas on and get ready for bed." Ryan was home alone once again and it felt weird. She was so used to King being there that she didn't think she could ever get used to him not being there. He was her lifeline and she had fucked it all up over a stupid mistake. If only she had never stopped to talk to Imran that day in the mall then she wouldn't be in the position she was in now. Ryan could only hope things would get better.

The twins were already sleeping and Cameron had just gone up. She needed some time to herself. She had a lot to think about. Ryan had to talk to Imran and find out who was working with him. She needed to know who was inside her house that was able to put a camera there.

Ryan was sitting in the family room with the music playing low. She had her wine and a blunt. She hadn't smoked since before she was pregnant with Cameron but she needed this because she was stressed to the max. As she listened to Tamar sing about staying and fighting she thought about King. The song described what she was feeling about her and King's situation. The words had so much meaning to them.

"We could walk away from this mess we made / We could live and learn, set fire to this bridge and watch it burn / We can act like it was not even really love in the first place."

Ryan sung along with the song and the tears fell. She was in such a state of confusion. She knew she had messed up but how could someone who professed to love her so much just walk away without a fight? *Did he really love me?* she questioned herself.

King sat outside the house he shared with Ryan. It was late but he missed her, plus he hadn't had any pussy in a minute. He craved Ryan and wanted nothing more than to slide up in her. He finally decided to go inside. He let himself in and heard music playing in the family room. When he walked in Ryan was laid back on the couch and her robe was slightly open, revealing part of her breasts. *Damn, she fine as hell*, he thought. King walked over to Ryan and sat down. She was so deep in thought that she never heard him enter the house.

"Hey, King. I didn't hear you come in." He responded by pulling her into his arms and she didn't resist.

"Ma, I miss the hell out of you but this shit is fucking with my head."

"I know. I'm so sorry for all this. I should have never talked to another man. We're supposed to be celebrating being husband and wife yet we're separated already." A tear fell down her face. She was in a vulnerable state and didn't know what was going on between her and King.

King lifted her face so that she was looking at him. He kissed her and she reciprocated it. It felt good to be in his arms, even if it was for a minute. The sad part was Ryan knew that he'd be leaving and they'd be right back where they were before he came over. But she needed him to make her feel good.

"I need you, King." He heard her and he needed her just as much. Ryan did something to him that no other woman ever did. He had a certain need for her. He had a craving that only she could fulfill. He pulled her on top of him and pushed her robe all the way off, fully exposing her caramel breasts. He took each nipple in his mouth one at a time and that made Ryan shudder. That was her spot and he knew it.

"Stand up, Ma, and strip." Ryan did as she was commanded. That turned King on. She had not one stretch mark or piece of fat and King loved it.

"He stood up and pulled her naked body to his. He just held on to her for a minute before his hands began to caress her body. Ryan was just as hungry for him as he was for her. She unzipped his pants and pulled out his dick. Her small hands on his dick made him grow to full length and he was ready.

"Come on, let's go upstairs, Ma." She turned and headed for the bedroom that they used to share and he followed. Ryan laid on the bed and began playing with her clit because she knew what King liked. She was the true definition of a woman in the streets but a freak in the sheets.

"Move those hands, Ma. I want to be the only one pleasing you." King dropped his pants and boxers before joining her in the bed. He started feasting on her breasts and made a trail down to her belly button and then to her thighs. He kissed the inside of each thigh and then dove head first inside her pussy. She was wet and waiting.

King loved her pussy. It always tasted sweet and was always wet.

"Oh shit, King!" Ryan was on the verge of cumming and that made King lick harder.

"Yup, cum all in Daddy's mouth." King used his finger along with his tongue to bring Ryan to her first climax of the night.

"Fuck! I'm cumming!" Ryan's eyes rolled in the back of her head as King replaced his tongue with his dick. He began pumping slow like he was making love to her. Ryan loved it slow and then fast.

"You like that shit, Ma?" he asked as he moved in and out of her.

"Yes, Daddy, I love it," she responded as she matched his rhythm. One thing Ryan could do was keep up with King during sex. Ryan was definitely a beast in the bed. King pulled out of her and Ryan looked at him like he was crazy.

"Get on top, Ma. I want to see you ride this dick." Ryan complied. Once she climbed on top his dick instantly slid inside of her and she went to work. One would think she was a professional cowgirl the way she

26

rode him. King tried to slow her down but Ryan was in her own zone and before he knew it his seeds had shot all up in her. That was probably some of the best sex that they had ever had. They had released all the pent up stress that they both had and were now relaxed. But how long before the bullshit returned?

Ryan woke up sore the next morning. She tried to shield her eyes from the sun that was shining brightly through the blinds. Once she focused and saw that she was lying naked under the sheets she realized that last night had really happened between her and King. But where was he? She got up and headed to the bathroom to relieve herself. Once she was done she grabbed her robe and headed to look for King. She looked everywhere in the house and there was no trace of him. Damn. He had pulled a hit it and quit it on her. Ryan felt stupid. She couldn't believe that King had treated her like this. This only made her realize that maybe they did need to go their separate ways. Yeah, she fucked up but she wasn't going to play games with King's ass. She was not about to be his booty call. This was truly the end for her and King.

Chapter Three

I'm Moving On

King and Ryan hadn't spoken to each other since the night they had sex two weeks ago. She had been communicating through Mia and Harlem. When he wanted the kids she'd drop them off to Mia and pick them up through her as well. She felt that King had played with her emotions and she didn't have time for it. It was time to move on. When she got with King it was the best time of her life and never in a million years did she think that they'd be over, but it seems as though it had come to just that.

It was King's weekend with the kids and Ryan felt the need to get out of the house. She had been moping around and feeling bad but she was done. If King couldn't forgive her and move on then fuck it. She was dressed to kill in her all black bustier with pink studs all over the breasts. She wore a black mini skirt and all black Louboutins with pink studs on the heels. She had her hair straight down her back with a part in the middle and was ready to hit the town. Her girls Tracy and Chrissy were meeting her at Ace of Spades.

When Ryan pulled up to the club it was packed and she was ready to have some fun. Ace of Spades was a strip club but that's where everyone hung if they weren't at King's club. After parking the car she headed inside to meet her girls.

"Hey ladies!" Ryan greeted Chrissy and Tracy.

What's good, bitch? I'm surprised to see you out and about," Chrissy said as she took a gulp of her drink.

"Well I am and I'm ready to party," Ryan said as she flagged the waitress down.

"Don't look now but ya' baby daddy just walked in the building," said Tracy. Ryan turned to the door and damn near shit bricks. *What the fuck is he doing here?* she thought.

"I see my boys RBM have walked through the motherfuckin' door and y'all know they spend money. So all you broke niggas make room!" the DJ shouted out King and his group.

"What the hell is he doing here? I was trying to have a good time," Ryan said as she tried to stay out of King's site.

"Well, let's enjoy our time. Fuck him, girl," Chrissy replied. The girls continued to enjoy themselves when an up and coming hustler named Prince approached their table.

"Excuse me, Miss Lady, can I have a moment of your time?" Prince asked Ryan.

"Uh, yeah." She figured why not? She wasn't with King anymore and she was ready to live her life. They walked off to another table where they were alone. Unbeknown to Ryan, King had been watching her every move and he was pissed. Yeah, he left after they had sex but she was still his wife and needed to act like it.

"So you gone let ya wife just sit with that nigga Prince?" Harlem whispered in King's ear. He was the only other person that knew King and Ryan were married.

"Fuck her, man. I'm good. We ain't together," King stated even though he felt differently inside. He took shot after shot of Hennessy and a few blunts.

He watched Ryan walk away with Prince. They made their way to the dance floor and Prince's hands were all over Ryan. Even though he said he didn't care, he did. He watched Ryan dance provocatively on Prince and his blood boiled. He walked right over to Ryan and snatched her up.

"King, what the hell are you doing?!" Ryan couldn't believe King was dragging her off the dance floor. He took her to a corner where no one was.

"So you out here showing yo' ass like you single and shit." She gave him the side eye.

"Nigga, I am! Yo' ass ain't at home. Hell, you haven't been in what two months? Miss me with that bullshit."

"You know what, you wanna act like a ho then do you." King walked away pissed. He didn't even stop to say bye to his boys. He just headed out of the club.

It was the end of the night he was feeling himself. He decided to call up April, the chick he used to fuck with before Ryan came into the picture. If she wanted to play games then so would he. He headed to pick April up and take her to the room. He needed his dick sucked.

When he got to April's house she came right out and they headed to the room. Before he could even pull off all the way she had his dick out and was hitting him off. He didn't feel bad at all being as though Ryan was checking for other niggas. *She doing her so fuck it,* he thought.

Ryan and Prince hit it off and she actually wanted to kick it with him again so they exchanged numbers with the promise of hooking up later. After a night of fun they headed their separate ways. Ryan didn't feel an ounce of remorse because she was single, right? She would soon find out how King got down for real.

Chapter Four

New Beginnings, Sour Endings

A whole month had passed and Ryan and Prince were getting to know each other. She still hadn't spoken to King and surprisingly, she didn't care. At first she thought going out with Prince was temporary until King got his shit together, but the more time they spent together the more she liked him. Today they were going to the park for a picnic. This was something she never did with King so she was excited about it. Prince was really starting to win her over.

Ryan put the finishing touches on her makeup and gave herself the once over. She approved of her simple but cute look. She was glad King had the kids this weekend because she was free to do her. She headed out to meet Prince at the park, hoping to have a good time.

~ ~ ~ ~

King was spending time with his kids which he loved. The twins were getting bigger and crawling now. Cameron had starting asking questions about why King wasn't in the house and, truth be told, King had no idea what to tell him. He would just try to change the subject and so far it was working.

Today they were chilling with his mom which is where King had been staying since the breakup.

"So Cam, what do you want to do today?" King asked as they ate lunch.

"I don't know," he said while looking to be in deep thought.

"How about we make it a movie night? We can have popcorn and snacks and we can even pick Harlem Jr. up." That got him excited because he and Harlem's son had become really close.

"Yeah, and we can play video games, too." King just laughed. The joys of being a father.

Ryan was enjoying herself at the park but little did she know this fairytale would be short lived because Prince's true colors would soon show.

"So what's the deal with you and homeboy?" Prince wanted to know where King and Ryan's relationship stood. He was feeling her and was ready to move forward in their relationship. Ryan was a bad bitch and he was on his way to the top. Why not have a bad bitch by his side? Soon RBM would be a distant memory once Prince and his people took over.

"Well, we're not together as of now and I really don't see us getting back together. We've been separated for almost three months."

Prince was shocked. He had no idea they were married.

"Wait, let me get this straight; you're married to this nigga and he's acting up?" Ryan shook her head.

"Damn, Ma, so what does this mean for us? I mean since you're married and all." Prince was really trying to get on Ryan's good side. He had an infatuation with her and wasn't ready to let her go back to King. Period.

"Well, I like you and I think things are going good. So let's just take it one day at a time and see what happens."

"I can dig that, Ma, but just know that you're mine now and I'm not letting that nigga step on my toes." Ryan just smiled, thinking nothing of the comment when she really should have been running away from Prince. That was her warning sign but she was so wrapped up in how good he was treating her that she didn't pay attention to the warnings. She'd soon regret it.

RICH BOY MAFIA 2
DEMETTREA

Chapter Five

The Whole Truth and Nothing but the Truth

Ryan and Prince had been going strong for a good two months. She was still dropping the kids off to Mia who would take them to King, but not today. King had showed up to his brother's house to wait for Ryan. His son had told him some shit that he didn't want to believe. But he was about to get some answers from Ryan today.

He was sitting on the porch when she pulled up. She wasn't paying attention and never saw him sitting there.

"What's up, wife?" Ryan waved and tried to continue past him but he stopped her.

"Go ahead and take the kids inside and then step on back out here so we can talk."

"What is it that we need to talk about, King?" He gave her a look that said he wasn't playing so she proceeded into the house. Two minutes later she came back out.

"So that nigga be disrespecting you in front of my son?" Ryan's face told the whole story. She wasn't surprised that Cameron had told King about Prince.

"Nah, we just got into and Cam heard us. It's not that serious." King bit the inside of his jaw. He didn't know what to say.

"I never took you for a weak woman, Ryan, but know that I will bury that nigga alive if he steps out of line." She shook her head in understanding. Little did King know she needed him, but her pride wouldn't let her tell him that. She was afraid of what he might think.

"He stood up and walked in the house, leaving Ryan on the porch alone. He knew there was more to the story but he didn't have a clue. So for now he'd leave it alone.

~ ~ ~ ~

King walked in the house just as Ryan was getting dressed. She was leaned over, fastening the strap of her Alexander McQueen shoes. King watched her backside and his dick jumped. Ryan had been dating Prince and it was going pretty well. King had heard all about dude and he felt some type of way. Even though he and Ryan weren't together anymore he still considered her his.

"Where the hell you going?" he asked, startling her.

What the hell, King! Make some damn noise next time, nigga."

"Whatever, man. Answer the damn question." He had a vein popping out of his forehead and Ryan thought it was cute that he was a little jealous.

"Uh, excuse you! I'm grown and single."

"Don't get homeboy fucked up." With that he walked out of the room. Ryan shook her head at King's behavior. He wasn't ready to be with her, yet he didn't want anyone else to be with her. She loved King but he had to get his shit together. The world didn't revolve around King Pierre.

King on the other hand felt that they were just on a break. Hell, she was his fucking wife. No one knew but them because they had snuck off to the courthouse and got married the day after he asked her. Not even a few days after, all the drama happened which caused them to not even enjoy their nuptials.

King shook his head as he thought about the day he gave Ryan his last name. Here it is, now six months later, and they should have been planning the ceremony with friends and family but instead they were separated and possibly headed for divorce.

Ryan walked towards the door and past King. She was meeting Prince at the movies being that this was King's home and she'd never disrespect him by bringing another man there. She was looking forward to a good night with Prince. He was definitely winning her over.

~ ~ ~ ~

It was 2 AM when Ryan got home. She had really enjoyed herself with Prince. It was dark so she assumed that King had left plus his car was gone.

"Oh shit, King! What the hell are you doing sitting up in the dark?" As soon as she had opened the door he was sitting there in the foyer with a blunt in his hand.

"Did you fuck him?" Ryan was taken aback by his question.

"You have some fucking nerve, King. You don't want me but as soon as someone else shows interest in me you act crazy. I'm tired of this shit with you!" Tears had begun to fall. She had thought going out with Prince would open his eyes but it didn't.

"You sick of this shit but you're the one that fucked up – not me. But don't get it twisted, Ma, you're still my fucking wife. You need to dead that shit with my mans."

"Are you fucking serious? You out here doing you so I'm doing me. Fuck you, King!" Before the words were out of her mouth King had grabbed her by the collar of her shirt.

"Don't fucking play with me, Ryan. That nigga will be missing by tomorrow morning if you don't get rid of him." He let her go and walked out the house. Ryan slid to the floor and cried. She couldn't understand why King was acting like this. They hadn't been together as a couple in over six months.

King sat in his car in the garage and thought about how he was acting. Was he wrong? He couldn't help it when it came to Ryan. Maybe it was time for him to get his shit together and go home. Yeah she fucked up but it was obvious he couldn't shake her. That was his heart and he was ready to make shit right.

That night Ryan cried herself to sleep. She loved King but it seemed as if their relationship had caused her nothing but turmoil. How much more could she take from King?

~ ~ ~ ~

King sat in disbelief as he read the papers he had received in the mail. He couldn't believe that Ryan had really served him divorce papers. He wasn't ready to let go. He was ready to fight for his family but it may have been too late. He hadn't told Ryan yet, but he had hired an investigator because everything that happened between them seemed suspicious, especially the cameras being in their home. He had found out who was responsible; Tish. Not only that but she had been seen with Imran and that didn't sit well with him. He already knew what had to be done but he wanted his wife to know that he was over it and wanted to come home. He wanted to tell her how sorry he was for acting an ass without thinking. He never gave her the opportunity to explain the video. Instead, he acted on emotion and that may have cost him his family.

Sending those papers was the hardest thing Ryan ever had to do. She fought with herself long and hard about it but it seemed as if King didn't want her and Prince wasn't going anywhere, even though she was getting tired of him already. As Ryan was walking in the door her phone rang. She rolled her eyes when she realized it was Prince.

"Hello?" she answered with a bit of irritation in her voice.

"Where the hell you at?" he barked through the phone. He had become real possessive over the last few months.

"At home. Why?" Ryan had been thinking about packing up her kids and moving far away from all the bull.

"Don't fucking play with me, Ryan. I need you at my house pronto. A nigga hungry."

"Okay, Prince." With that Ryan hung up. She had to come up with a plan to get away from him. Truth be told, she was scared of him. He had a crazy side that Ryan had the pleasure of seeing once before. Ryan took a minute for herself before gathering her things to head over to Prince's house. Thank god Mia had picked the kids up earlier and they wouldn't be back until later on.

She didn't want her son to see Prince disrespect her again. The fairytale that she had experienced early in their relationship had turned into a nightmare.

"See, I told yo' dumb ass to go home to ya' wife. Now look at you sitting up here pouting and shit because she done served ya' ass papers. I don't feel bad for you, King. You have a wild ass temper and you jump to conclusions before you think. Now you got another nigga trying to take ya' spot. Dumb ass." Harlem wasn't being nice at all. He actually thought Ryan was good for his brother but King had to learn how to control his temper. He was always too quick to react without thinking, which wasn't a good thing. Harlem had no problem telling him he was wrong at all.

"Man, ain't nobody trying to hear that shit. She had no business talking to that nigga at all. If she would have never been grinning in his face we wouldn't be going through this shit. You not about to blame me for this shit," King spat back even though deep down he felt he was partially to blame.

"You young niggas gone learn, but I guess you will learn the hard way." With that Harlem walked away from King. He couldn't believe how stupid he was being. King sat and thought about what his brother had said. He thought about Ryan and his kids. There was no way he was signing those papers. He was about to get his family back.

"Did you give him the papers?" Prince asked Ryan. He had forced her to serve King with divorce papers even though she didn't want to. She prayed that King didn't sign them.

"Yeah," She said with a little bit too much attitude for Prince. Before Ryan knew what had happened he smacked her.

"Watch ya' damn tone with me. I ain't that soft ass nigga King. Now come take a ride with me," Prince told Ryan.

"Nah, you go ahead. I'm going to go pick up my kids." If looks could kill Ryan would have been dead.

"I wasn't asking you. I was telling you. Now let's go." Prince was headed to pick up some money and wanted Ryan with him. He didn't trust leaving her alone for fear that King might talk her out of filing for a divorce. It took him too long to get her to file the papers. So far everything was working in his favor. He had King's bitch and now he was about to claim his throne in the streets.

Ryan stood up and followed Prince to the car. She had been plotting on how to get away from him. She'd had enough of his controlling ways. It had gotten so bad that he was hitting on her now and that was something she was not going to tolerate. She'd be in jail for killing his ass before she let him continue to beat her.

"Where are we going?" she asked as they pulled off.

"I gotta pick up some money." She rolled her eyes.

"You know damn well I don't like riding with you while you do your dirt. Nigga, I have kids and I can't afford to be locked up behind your bullshit." Prince never got a chance to respond because as they pulled to a stop light shots were fired and when it was all said and done Ryan was slumped over. Prince had been hit but because he had on a bullet proof vest his injuries were minor. A bullet had gone in and out of his arm. Ryan wasn't so lucky. She had been hit twice. One bullet went through her arm and into her side, puncturing her lung and cracking her rib.

"Oh shit." Prince knew Ryan needed help but he also knew he couldn't be there when the police arrived. He decided to leave the scene and call the ambulance anonymously. He had a pretty good idea who was shooting at him and he was ready for revenge. The D-Boyz were in for a rude awakening.

When King got the call that Ryan had been shot his heart broke in two. He couldn't believe that this shit was happening. It took a minute to get himself together before going to the hospital.

"Are you good, man?" Harlem asked. All of King's boys from RBM were there as well as all of King's and Ryan's family with the exception of the kids.

"Yeah, man, but that nigga is dead on everything. I know he had something to do with her getting shot. I told her to leave that nigga alone but she didn't listen. I know how Prince gets down and he has plenty of enemies." Harlem just shook his head. He had to prepare himself because he knew King and he wasn't letting this go. He was out for blood.

King walked into the room and saw Ryan hooked up to all kinds of shit and he broke down. King portrayed a hard exterior on the outside but when it came to Ryan he was soft. He realized at that moment just how much he needed her in his life. The saying was definitely true; you don't know what you have until it's gone. And now that he was losing Ryan he knew he wanted her and was prepared to do what he needed to make it happen.

"Damn, Ma, how did we come to this point? We were supposed to be happy and celebrating our marriage. Not on the verge of a divorce. I need you here with me, Ma. A nigga ready to get his shit together. Just don't leave me, Ma. I can't do this shit without you." King wiped the tear that had fallen from his eye. It hurt him to the core to see his love lying in the hospital. King vowed right then and there that Prince would pay. He hated himself for being so selfish and not working out their differences. Ryan was right when she said he acted without facts. He never once thought about the fact that there was a camera in their home without his knowledge. That night King stayed by Ryan's side hoping for a full recovery.

~ ~ ~ ~

Prince wanted to go to the hospital but he knew King was there and he didn't want those problems. He had an inside resource keeping him updated on Ryan's condition. No matter how he treated her, he cared for her. He wouldn't go as far as to say he loved her but there was something there. Or maybe it was the thrill of having something that belonged to King. He got a hard on just thinking about Ryan. He had to relieve it soon too because Ryan had yet to let him sample the goods. He was growing real impatient with her. Even though he got her to send King divorce papers, Prince could tell that she was still wrapped up in King. That was something he had to get a handle on. Bottom line was he wanted to be in King's position in every aspect and was willing to do whatever to get there. What Prince didn't know was that King had someone trailing his every move. He was so wrapped up in taking King's spot that he forgot the number one rule; always be aware of your surroundings.

Ryan had woke up after a week but no one on the outside was to know. King didn't want whoever shot her trying to finish the job even though he thought the bullets were meant for Prince. He had a source tell him the D-Boyz were behind it but it had yet to be confirmed.

King sat in the chair with his head in his hands. He was beyond stressed. He hadn't slept much in the past week because of his worry for Ryan.

"King?" Ryan called out. He immediately looked up.

"What's up, Ma? You need something?" he asked. He had been catering to her every need.

"Yeah, I need to use the bathroom." Ryan felt handicapped. She hated having to depend on King. What she didn't know was King was ready to be what she needed and more. He had realized his fuck-ups and was man enough to admit it.

"Come on, Ma." King helped Ryan stand to her feet and walked her to the bathroom. Once she was in there he stood there and waited.

"You don't have to stand there. I'll call you when I'm done." She didn't want to feel like a burden to him but what she didn't understand was no matter what they went through he'd always be there for her.

"Nah Ma, I got you." When she was done King helped her back to bed."

"Are you thirsty or hungry?" he asked her.

"Nah, but I want to see my babies." King didn't think it was a good idea for the kids to come to the hospital. Especially Cameron. He would ask too many questions that King didn't want to answer.

"Well, let's see when their releasing you and then we'll go from there. I really don't want my kids up here at the hospital. Ryan shook her head even though she still just wanted her kids. They were the only ones that loved her without judgment.

"Don't look like that, Ma. I'm here and I'm not going anywhere, I promise. We're going to get past all this shit and get back to us. I miss you and my kids and a nigga fucked up. I shouldn't have reacted so quick without all the facts. It's just that with you I'm so fucking territorial and to see someone else hands on you drives me crazy. To even think of you with another nigga...It's just something I can't fathom." Ryan just looked at King in silence. She really didn't know what to say. She loved this man with everything in her but could they work out their differences? Only time would tell if love would withstand all.

Chapter Six
I'll Never Leave You Alone

Imran was going over the documents that he had received. He was in shock that Ryan had been shot. He didn't know all the details but he knew he had to get at whoever did it. He would do anything for Ryan. His infatuation for her ran deep and all he wanted was to have her by his side as his woman. King didn't deserve her. He was too neglectful and didn't realize what he had, but Imran would gladly show him.

He looked at the picture of Ryan and his dick began to swell. He pulled his dick out and began to masturbate to the pic. It was just something about Ryan that had him gone. He jerked off, imagining that it was Ryan's hands and within minutes he was cumming all over the pic. Yeah, he had to get the real thing.

It was time for Ryan to go home and she was more than happy. She was ready for a hot shower and her big comfortable bed. Sleeping in the hospital bed was no joke. King had pulled out all the stops to make sure her transition was smooth. He hired a massage therapist, a cook, and as gave Consuela more hours. He didn't want her to have to do anything.

When they pulled up to the house he helped her inside.

"You want to go upstairs or do you want to chill in the den?" King asked her.

"I think I want to shower and then get in the bed. My body is real sore from that bed."

"Well, I hired a massage therapist so just say the word and I'll call her up." Ryan smiled at King's thoughtfulness.

"Okay, thanks." King bent down and kissed her forehead before leaving her to shower. He headed down to the kitchen where Marco, the chef he hired, was.

"Hey Marco, cook something simple for the Mrs. She isn't hungry now but I have a feeling she will be soon."

"Sure thing, Mr. Pierre." Marco was a five-star chef who has cooked for many celebrities and came highly recommended. He wanted the best for his family, especially in this time of recovery for Ryan. King made a call to Mia and told her to keep the kids another day to give Ryan some time to relax.

"You know I got you, bro, but this time don't run away from y'all problems. Face them head on. You two were meant for each other but you have to stop being so damn fast to react, King." He knew everything Mia was saying was true.

"Yeah, I hear you sis." He was working on getting his shit together for his family.

"Love you, bro. Tell Ryan to get some rest and I love you guys." King was grateful for Mia. She had become such an amazing support system for him since she married his brother. *Harlem is one lucky bastard,* King thought as he headed up to check on his wife.

Tish couldn't believe King was back at home with Ryan. She had worked too hard to break them up for him to just go back. She had been following Ryan around and thought she had moved on with Prince, only to see King back with her now.

"What the fuck does this bitch have to make these niggas keep coming back? Hmph, I bet that shit won't last long." What King never knew was that Tish had been diagnosed with bipolar disorder as a child and recently she had even began talking to herself and cutting her wrist. Tish pulled away from King's house with a plan. Hopefully this one wouldn't backfire. Just like Prince, she had no idea that she was being watched as well. King didn't trust anyone, and after that ordeal at his home with Ryan and Imran he made sure everybody that was suspect to him was watched. Most people knew King was that nigga but only a few really knew. He had just had a meeting with his accountant who helped him clean up a lot of his money and to date King's net worth was 3.2 billion and not even his brother knew that. He was a self-made billionaire.

~ ~ ~ ~

"Damn Mia, you trying to kill a nigga." Mia had walked in Harlem's office in nothing but a thong and a pair of gold Giuseppe Zanotti suede snake heels. Her perky breasts sat up straight and her nipples poked out, begging to be sucked. Harlem instantly got a hard on. One thing he loved about his wife was her willingness to please him. She knew how hard he worked and was always waiting at home with a hot meal, a blunt, and some freaky sex. He couldn't get enough of Mia.

"Well, I knew you had been in here working and thought you could use a break, Daddy." Mia walked over to Harlem and straddled him. Her nipples were directly in front of his mouth. He took the left one in his mouth while twirling the other between his thumbs. The soft moans from Mia made his dick grow even more. He needed to be inside of her. He stood her up and dropped his pants and boxers. He roughly pushed her over his desk and ripped her thong off before entering her. Mia liked when he was rough. It turned her on.

"Damn Ma, yo' shit wet as fuck." Harlem went in and out while Mia threw it back. The sex between the two was amazing.

"Shit bae, I'm about to cum!" Mia yelled. She was on the verge of a mind-blowing orgasm that nobody could give her but Harlem. He was hitting walls that she didn't even know existed.

"Come on Ma, let's cum together." If Mia wasn't on birth control she probably would have gotten pregnant from that session.

"Damn Ma, you are definitely the truth." Harlem said as he smacked her on the ass before they retreated to their room for round two.

King was out handling business. He had to pick up money and then he'd be headed home to chill with Ryan. He had been doing better with coming home at a decent time. They hadn't been sleeping in the same bed, but they were cordial with each other. Tonight he wanted to do something nice for her so he ordered pink roses, which were her favorite, and he had the chef prepare lobster, shrimp, and steak. He wanted to show her that he wanted her and that he was past the events that happened. He even went to the jeweler earlier that week and had her a new ring made. He wanted the night to go perfect. He knew Ryan had her doubts about their relationship, but tonight he wanted to erase them all.

When King pulled up to Javon's house he was already waiting.

"What up, man?" Javon greeted him as he got in the car.

"Ain't shit. Just ready to get this over with so I can get back to the wife. I got a special evening planned for her." Javon was happy that King and Ryan got their shit together. They were made for each other and he hated to see them apart for so long.

"That's what's up, but aye tell Ryan to hook me up with her girl Chrissy." King laughed at him as he pulled into traffic.

"What's funny, nigga? Shit, she bad as hell with her bowlegged ass."

"Man please, you gone have Trina after yo' ass and hers," King replied.

"Yeah, well let me worry about Trina's ass. Plus I'm tired of the drama with her. I haven't even really been staying there and I started moving my shit out the house." King turned to Javon.

"Damn bruh, shit sounds serious." Javon had always been with Trina, so to see him without her was unnatural.

"Hell yeah." King saw the seriousness in Javon's face and knew his friend was done. He just hoped that Trina didn't make it hard for him to leave. He knew Javon would take care of his seed, and Trina for that matter, but Trina was known for drama.

"Well, if you need something man, just let me know." King offered.

"I told you what I needed; Chrissy's fine ass." They laughed as they headed to their destination.

When they pulled up to the house on Strathmore, Javon went in and collected while King waited in the car.

"What's up, Peanut? Y'all got the money ready?"

"Yeah, it's all ready to go but that nigga Gutter was short again. We went to collect from him and he was three hundred dollars short. I told him King wasn't gone be too happy." Javon shook his head. Gutter had been late the last two times and Javon hadn't told King. Instead he handled it himself, but this time he had to tell the boss. What would happen to Gutter was up in the air because no one knew what mood King was in, but they all knew what he was capable of.

"Well, give what you have and as far as Gutter goes that's the boss' call." Peanut headed towards the back of the house to retrieve the duffle bag full of money. He shook his head as he came back. He didn't want to be in Gutter's shoes. One thing you didn't do was mess with King's money. King was very generous and broke bread with you as long as you remained loyal and didn't fuck up, but he didn't play games either. Javon grabbed the duffle bag from Peanut and headed for the door. When he got back in the car he looked at King, not ready to deliver the news about Gutter.

"Why the fuck you looking at me like that?" King asked. He knew something was up but he didn't know what.

"Man, it's Gutter. He was short again." King looked at Javon with a look of confusion.

"What the fuck you mean again?" King's blood was boiling. He couldn't believe Javon hadn't told him that Gutter was fucking up.

"Man, he was short once before but I handled it because I knew you was dealing with personal shit. But this is the second time." King didn't say anything else as he pulled off headed to where Gutter was known to hang. He was about to make an example out of him so that everyone else would know the consequences of messing with his money.

When King pulled up to the trap on Marlowe, he hopped out, leaving the car running. Just as King thought Gutter was posted with Paco and Reese, two of King's workers. They were chilling as if they didn't have shit to do and that only made King madder. They weren't even on guard; a surefire way for the jack boys to get at them. They were in for a rude awakening, though. King was about to shut shit down. He walked right up to Gutter with a look that said *You know you fucked up, right?*

"Where the fuck is my money?

"Uh…" Gutter hesitated. King never gave him a chance to finish as his fist connected with Gutter's jaw. The impact was so great that those nearby heard it crack.

"Yo' ass is done! Get the fuck off my block!" He turned to the rest of the crew. "Y'all mothafuckas get back to work before everybody be out of a job." King walked back to the car and got in. They had one more spot to go to before going to count.

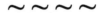

Ryan had started to heal pretty well and was able to get around without help. The kids were back home and she was happy. Her and King were on speaking terms even though they hadn't fully gotten back to the way things were. He still catered to her and did things for her like making sure she had a bath ready or a massage. He made sure that the chef prepared every meal so that she didn't have to do a lot.

Ryan was sitting in the den with Chasity asleep across her lap. As she watched her sleep she saw just how much she favored King. Only thing the twins possessed of Ryan was her skin color. One thing she was grateful for was that she gave King babies. If they ever did split up, at least she'd have a part of him.

"Ma, what you still doing up?" Ryan looked up at King in the doorway. She was so wrapped up in Chasity that she didn't hear him come in.

"I got tired of sitting up in the bed. I needed a change of scenery." King walked over and picked Chasity up from Ryan's lap.

"I'm going to go lay her down and then we can watch a movie or something." Ryan smiled. They were getting on the right track. She just hoped that they stayed there. King headed upstairs to lay Chasity in her bed and checked on Christian as well as Cameron. They all were out and probably would be for the rest of the night.

King headed to the guest room where he had been sleeping to change into a pair of basketball shorts. He was tired and just wanted to chill with Ryan. He had forgiven her for the incident with Imran even though he still didn't know all the details surrounding it. However, he did have someone looking in to it. He had found several cameras placed throughout the house and had them removed as well as checked for prints and anything that he could think of. He had to know who was fucking with his family.

After he was comfortable, he headed downstairs where Ryan was waiting for him. Ryan fought hard to keep her composure. Seeing King in nothing but a pair of shorts had her gone. His ripped muscles were bulging out and Ryan was leaking. Even when she was mad at him her body wasn't.

"Stop staring, Ma. You look thirsty." Ryan rolled her eyes and threw a couch pillow at him.

"Whatever, punk. You're the one coming down here half naked and shit." King just smiled as he sat next to Ryan and pulled her close to him.

"I love you, Ma." King said as he kissed the Ryan's forehead. Ryan didn't respond. They had been through so much in such a short time that she wasn't confident they would last. She just knew that something was waiting to blow up in her face. What, was the question?

Chapter Seven
Let's Get Married

Things had been going good for King and Ryan. He had been sleeping back in the bedroom that they shared. They had even started talking wedding plans again. The thing was, Ryan still had her doubts about them. She didn't want to but something wasn't sitting well with her and she couldn't pinpoint it.

Mia, Yvette, and Kita were over helping her plan the wedding.

"I can't believe y'all asses got married and didn't tell no damn body." Mia looked up at Ryan.

"Well, from what I hear you and Harlem did the same thing." Mia laughed.

"I guess I'm busted." The ladies laughed and cried and just enjoyed each other's company. Ryan was grateful to have them in her life. Even when she and King were on the outs they were still there for her.

"Well, I'm just happy y'all got it together. King can be hotheaded at times but one thing I know is that he loves him some Ryan," Yvette chimed in.

"Yes, honey. As long as I have known him, I've never seen him this close to a female. And he married yo' ass, so you know he loves you," Kita added. She was the hardcore one of the crew. She was married to Markie, one of Harlem's best friends. They had their share of issues, like cheating and being separated, but they overcame that and now they were the parents of two. Yvette was married to Harlem's best friend Tez and they had two kids.

"Well, I love his crazy ass, too," Ryan replied

"So Ryan, what ideas do you have for the wedding? I mean you're married to a boss so you got to have a boss ass wedding." There was Kita again with her ghetto talk.

"Girl, I have no clue. I just want something simple. I mean we're already married but I feel like I cheated my mom and you all out of the experience. So I want to have something small and simple," Ryan replied.

"Well, no worries; we got ya back. This weekend we can go shopping for dresses and look at a few venues," Mia offered.

"Sounds like a plan." Ryan stood up and turned on the stereo and Tamar Braxton crooned through the speakers. The ladies sipped wine and talked shit for the rest of the night. They had a bond that would forever be.

~ ~ ~ ~

So that nigga wanna play tough, huh?" King asked. He was seated at the head of the table in what they called the boardroom. Every week RBM had meetings. King had to make sure everyone stayed on their toes. The smallest mishap could cause an empire to fall, and right now they had a weak link within the dynasty.

"We can't afford any weak links so with that being said, you all know what has to be done." Everyone nodded their heads in agreement with King. Gutter had been talking real greasy about what he was going to do to King. He was pissed that King had embarrassed him in front of everyone.

"Now that we all are on the same page, I'm putting Javon in charge. I have some things coming up that I have to handle with the Mrs. and I need to make sure that this is handled.

"I got you, boss man," Javon replied. A few people in the room felt some kind of way about King's decision but they would never voice their opinions. King was the leader and they respected him even if they didn't agree with him.

"What about that Imran situation, boss?" Peanut asked.

"We'll handle that when I get back from vacation with my family. Trust that nigga ain't going no anywhere. I have a set of eyes on him at all times. Plus he too damn busy trying to sniff behind my wife and take what's mine. Trust his day is coming." King's phone rang and he looked at it and saw it was Ryan. He signaled for the crew to give him a minute.

"What's good, Ma?" Even though he was in a meeting, when Ryan called he took it. He never wanted her to feel neglected again. His family was his number one priority.

"I wanted to know what time you were coming home?"

"I'm wrapping up my meeting right now and I'm headed your way."

"Okay, cool. I was hoping we could go over the options for the venue and maybe do a menu for the wedding." King was willing to do whatever made Ryan happy, even though he would be happy with whatever she chose. But if she wanted him to have a part in the planning then he would.

"That's cool, Ma. Give me a few to wrap this up and I'll be there." They said their goodbyes and King continued with the meeting.

"Okay, back to business. Rahsaan, I need you to make sure everyone is paid and got what they need. Being that we'll be away and pretty much unreachable for a week I wanna make sure everything is set." King was planning a getaway with Ryan to Jamaica. She didn't know but it was the wedding of her dreams. Everyone would be there. Harlem and King's mom along with Consuela were going to look after the kids while they were in Jamaica. He wanted to spend some much-needed time with his wife. He wanted to get to know her all over again. He needed to see what he saw in her in the beginning. And in order for that to happen he had to get completely away from business.

"I got you, man. Now get home to wifey 'cause it sound like she'd ready for you to bring that ass." They all laughed.

"Alright, I'm officially on vacation. If anybody needs anything call Javon." King headed out the door, anxious to get to his wife.

Ryan was at home getting the twins ready for bed when King walked through the door.

"Hey, babe," she said as he grabbed her from behind.

"I missed the hell out of you." He kissed her neck and that made Ryan shudder. They hadn't been intimate in almost eight months. They were separated for six and the last two were spent getting back right. Ryan was horny and ready and so was King.

"Well, I almost got her to sleep and then I'm yours. For some reason this little girl never wants to go to bed on time. I have no problems with Christian but Chasity likes to stay up late." King released Ryan and picked Chasity up out of her bed.

"Go get showered and relax. Let Daddy take care of it." Ryan loved King as a father. He went above and beyond; even for Cameron who wasn't his biologically. That's something she'll be forever grateful for.

"Thanks, baby." She kissed his lips and made her way to the master bedroom.

When Ryan got out the shower King had the room set up for her. He had candles and massage oils ready. He had strawberries and champagne by the bedside. Tonight was all about Ryan. He wanted to please her and make her feel good.

"Come on over here and lay down, Ma. Let ya' man take care of you tonight." Ryan walked over and laid on her stomach. King hit play on the stereo and Lyfe Jennings blared through the speakers.

Must be nice having someone who understands the life you live/ must be nice having someone who's slow to take and quick to give/ must be nice having someone who sticks around when the rough times get thick/ someone who's smile is bright enough to make the projects feel like a mansion/ must be nice having someone who loves you despite your faults/ must be nice having someone who talks the talk but also walks the walk/ must nice having someone who understands that a thug has feelings too/ someone who loves you for sho'/ you just remember to never let 'em go

The words to that song had so much meaning behind them. Ryan was the chick that held him down without judgment. She didn't care about his money and

72

she was giving. She made sure the little things that he needed were done. King would forever be there for her.

King took the oil and poured it on her back, legs, and thighs. He started massaging her from her shoulders all the way to her ankles. Ryan was in heaven.

"Turn over, Ma." She did and King tried his best not to indulge in her body. She was flawless. He poured oil over the front of her body and massaged her from her breasts all the way to her toes. Once he saw that she was relaxed, he reached over and grabbed a strawberry and fed her.

"Mmm, that's good," Ryan moaned. She was relaxed and loved the romantic setting. Her pussy was on fire being that she hadn't had sex in a while. Her body was yearning for King.

King grabbed the champagne and poured it down the front of her body. He then licked every drop from her breasts to her navel.

"Tonight is all about you, Ma. You work hard with our kids and make sure we all are taken care of so it's time for Daddy to take care of you." Before Ryan could respond King was already nibbling on her clit. He found that Ryan was ready for him, just like he liked it. He sucked and licked her pussy until she begged for him to stop. He had made her cum at least three times and he hadn't even penetrated her yet. He didn't plan on it. He wanted her to be relaxed and taken care of but Ryan had other plans.

Once King was satisfied that Ryan was relaxed, he climbed next to her ready to cuddle but Ryan climbed on top of him. She pulled at his shorts and that turned him on. He loved it when she took control. Once his shorts and boxers were off, Ryan climbed on top and his dick instantly found her entrance. Ryan eased down slowly and began to ride him. This was King's favorite position. He loved to watch her breasts bounce around while she rode him like a cowgirl.

"Damn Ma, ride that shit." King smacked her on the ass and that made Ryan speed up. She was in her zone. King had that good dick that made you zone out. King too was hooked on Ryan's pussy. It was like she was made just for him. All nine inches fit her perfectly and her pussy stayed tight.

"You like that, Daddy?" Ryan asked seductively.

"Hell yeah, Ma. You doing ya' thang, baby. You already know what Daddy like." Ryan moved her hips in a circular motion while playing with her nipples.

"Damn bae, I'm about to cum!" she sang out." King grabbed hold of her hips and guided her. He wanted to cum with her.

"Shit, me too, Ma. Fuck!" King screamed out like a bitch but Ryan always did that to him. She was his drug of choice.

"Damn Ma, you trying to kill a nigga," King joked.

"Well, I'm the best at what I do. That's why you put a ring on it," Ryan joked back.

"Hell yeah. I had to cuff yo' fine ass." King smacked her on the ass. They cuddled and slept in each other's arms all night. This was the begging of a new foundation for the two that had been through so much. But as always, something was sure to interrupt their flow.

The day had finally come for King and Ryan's ceremony. Even though she was already his wife he wanted to give her the wedding of her dreams. She deserved it and so much more. Everyone that meant something to the two were in attendance. King had Mia find out what Ryan's dream wedding was and he made it happen. Mia was told to just make sure Ryan found a dress and showed up. While Ryan thought she was planning a small and simple gathering King went behind her back and planned the wedding that she really wanted. He knew Ryan was being modest and didn't want to make a big deal but he knew she'd also love the wedding of her dreams.

King spared no expense. He had the best caterers, security, and he even got Eric Benet and Tamia to sing. The colors that Ryan chose were turquoise and white.

King had flown everyone out to Jamaica and now they were on the beach awaiting the bridal party. When he heard Eric Benet start to sing King looked up and saw Harley and Madison coming towards him.

I never knew such a day could come/ and I never knew such a love could be inside me.

76

Harley and Madison made a path of flower petals from turquoise and white roses. Next came Cameron and Harlem each with a pillow and a ring on it. They had on white tuxes with turquoise shirts.

I never knew till I looked in your eyes I was incomplete till the day you walked into my life/ I never knew that my heart could feel so precious and pure/ one love so real.

It was time for Mia, Yvette, Kita, Chrissy, and Tracy to walk. Once the last person walked King felt the tear fall. Yeah, they were married already but this wedding was symbolic. It was special.

Can I just see you every morning when I open my eyes/ can I just feel your heart beating beside mine every night/ can we just feel this way together till the end of all time/ can I just spend my life with you?

Ryan was wearing an all-white lace and floral patterned strapless dress by Vera Wang. Her hair was in a bun and her high cheek bones were on display. Ryan was extremely beautiful. When she finally made it to Kings side the tears were falling. She loved this man with every beat of her heart. She was totally surprised at the wedding. When she was planning their wedding it was set for a week from today. She thought the trip to Jamaica was just a family trip. She had no idea that it was for her dream wedding. King had really outdone himself.

She remembered just an hour ago questioning Mia when she told her to get dressed in the wedding gown. Mia told her to hush and get dressed. She had a whole glam team to do her hair and make-up. And now, here she stood before her husband ready to say her vows to him.

The minister began. "Dearly beloved, we are gathered here today in the sight of God to witness and celebrate one of life's greatest moments; to give recognition to the worth and beauty of love and to add our best wishes and blessings to the union of King Pierre and Ryan Pierre. King and Ryan, marriage is an institution ordained by God, and is not to be entered into lightly or unadvisedly but reverently, deliberately, and only after much consideration. Coming together in marriage you are committing yourselves exclusively, to one another for as long as you both shall live. If you would turn to face one another and join hands as you each take your marital vows."

King looked into Ryan's eyes. "Ryan, you are the air that I breathe. I never thought I could love someone so much until I met you. You gave me purpose and you gave me my kids. I could never love another the way I love you."

Ryan wiped the tears from her eyes before she began. "King, before I met you I was lost. You came into my life at a time when I needed someone. You have showed me what it means to love. I can't imagine my life without you in it and I am happy to have you as my husband."

"What tokens of love do you have for each other?" King turned to get the ring from Harlem and Ryan from Mia.

"The wedding ring is an outward symbol, signifying to all the union of man and woman in holy matrimony. May the rings that you hold symbolize the nature of God in your lives and as often as either of you see them, may you be reminded of this moment and the endless love you have promised each other. King, as you present Ryan with her ring and pledge your love and your life to her, will you please repeat after me. I give you this ring as a symbol of my love. With all that I am and all that I have, I promise to love and honor you always. With this ring I thee wed." It was King's turn to repeat after the minister.

"Ryan, I give you this ring as a symbol of my love. With all that I am and all that I have, I promise to love and honor you always. With this ring I thee wed," King recited.

"Now Ryan, you repeat after me as well. I give you this ring as a symbol of my love. With all that I am and all that I have, I promise to love and honor you always. With this ring I thee wed."

"King, I give you this ring as a symbol of my love. With all that I am and all that I have, I promise to love and honor you always. With this ring I thee wed." They placed the rings on one another's fingers.

"You have consented to be joined together in holy matrimony, and having pledged and sealed your vows by giving and receiving rings in the presence of both God and family. It is with great pleasure that I now pronounce you husband and wife. What God has joined together, let no man put asunder. You may kiss the bride." King took Ryan in his arms and kissed her with so much passion, it was probably the most electrifying kiss ever.

"It is with great joy and honor that I present to you Mr. and Mrs. Pierre." Everyone clapped and got excited. They were happy to join King and Ryan at their wedding. There wasn't a dry eye in the audience. It was a new beginning for a union that would be unbreakable. Even when tested, what is meant to be will always be.

After the reception King took Ryan back to the Villa that they were staying in. He was horny and ready. Before they even got in the door all the way he was all over her.

"Damn Ryan, yo' shit stay wet." King was playing with her pussy and she was about to cum but he moved his hands. Ryan looked at him like he had two heads.

"Why the hell you stop, nigga?"

"Chill, Ma. I got you." King turned the Jacuzzi on so that he and Ryan could get in. He lit candles and grabbed a bottle of wine and two glasses.

"Come on, Ma," King called to Ryan when he came back out. He helped her out of her clothes and then they got in the Jacuzzi. King sat down and Ryan sat on his lap facing him. Ryan felt his dick get hard and that was her cue. She lifted up just a little so that she could fit his dick inside.

"Damn Ma, that shit is tight as fuck!" Ryan rode him slowly, savoring the feeling of him being inside of her. Sex with King was always mind-blowing. He had a gift when it came to laying the pipe. That night they went at it for damn near four hours.

******

"No, stop it! Get off me!" King woke up to Ryan fighting in her sleep.

"Ma, wake up." He didn't know what happened or what she was dreaming about but he didn't like it.

"You okay, Ma?" he asked, concerned.

"Um, yeah. I just had a bad dream," she responded. King was worried because she was drenched in sweat.

"You wanna talk about it?" he offered.

"Well, when I was little my father used to molest me. When I turned thirteen he tried to go even farther by penetrating me. Every once I a while I have nightmares about it." Ryan thought back to that night in her bedroom.

"Baby girl, come here to Daddy." Ryan hesitated before walking over to her daddy. She was just nine when he first started touching her and she thought what he was doing was okay because he was her daddy. Plus, he told Ryan that if she ever told anyone they'd never believe her. He went so far as to tell Ryan that her mom would put her out if she told. She believed him so she stayed quiet. Four years later it was still happening.

"You know Daddy loves you, right?" He looked at Ryan and she shook her head up and down. Tears were threating to fall from her innocent face, not knowing her father was about to try to take her innocence.

He stood up and walked Ryan over to the bed and laid her down. She had never been so scared in her life. Every other time he just fondled her, but this time it seemed to be going much further. Ryan stared at the ceiling and counted back from 10. She looked over at the trophy she had won in a cheer competition. Just as he was pulling her panties down she reached over and grabbed the trophy. Ryan hit him right in the back of his head before he even knew what had happened. When he reached for his head she kicked him off of her and ran. She ran straight out the door, never looking back. She ended up at a neighbor's house. She was a sweet old lady that loved all the kids in the neighborhood.

Ryan was out of breath and could barely talk. She tried to calm Ryan down and find out what happened. That's a night Ryan would never forget. Her mom ended up pressing charges on her father and they moved away. Ryan hadn't seen him since but that was something that stayed with her forever. Every once in a while she'd have those nightmares and she hated it.

"Damn, Ma." King pulled Ryan close to him. He never knew she had been through so much. He wanted to find her father and put two in him for what he had done to her.

"It's cool. I'm over it. It's just these damn nightmares." That night King held her in his arms all night and she felt safe.

Chapter Eight
The Calm Before the Storm

King had been chilling at home with his family a lot lately. He basically fell back and let Rahsaan and Javon run things, especially the record label. Since the incident with Imran they had severed all ties per their legal team. It wasn't a big issue, however, because King was well-known and they were able to start their own label, Skyy Records. Now that their honeymoon period was over King had to get back to the money.

King walked into Skyy Records like a boss. Everything about him screamed *I'm that nigga.*

"Good morning, Mr. Pierre," Candace, his secretary, spoke while passing him a cup of coffee and a folder of important documents.

"Morning, Candace," King replied as he headed to his office. He had to get back into the swing of things. Being off for two weeks had him comfortable. He was enjoying the time with his family but money had to made.

King's phone went off. It was a text from Ryan.

Wifey: I miss you, bae. Can't you work from home?

Me: Nah Ma, I got a lot to do but I won't be late.

Wifey: Okay. Love you.

Me: Love you, too, Ma

King was happy that they were able to get past their issues. Now he had to focus on the folder that sat in front of him. It contained the info he needed on Imran and who was working with him. It was time for some get back. He had disrespected King and his wife.

When King opened the folder he couldn't believe his eyes. He should have known Tish didn't go away that easily. He studied the photos of Imran and Tish meeting and his blood boiled. So the whole time she was plotting with Imran to come between King and Ryan. They obviously had forgotten who King was, but he was about to remind them. He closed the folder and sat there thinking. He had to be smart about the whole situation.

"Candace, please have Rahsaan and Javon meet me in the conference room," King said over the intercom.

The conference room was soundproof and he didn't need anyone hearing their conversation. Shit was about to get real. King gathered everything he needed and headed to the conference room where Javon and Rahsaan were already waiting. King closed and locked the door before sitting down.

"I found out that Tish and Imran have been working together, so you know what has to be done," King stated as he looked at his boys. He met with these two because he trusted them.

"So what do you need us to do?" Javon asked, ready to ride with whatever King wanted.

"Well, that nigga has an expiration date and it's a week from today. He won't live past that but we have to move smart. We plan and then we move, in silence." They wrapped up their meeting and King headed home to his wife.

~ ~ ~ ~

King was at the Pink Kitty chilling with RBM, something he hadn't done in quite some time. He had been enjoying the married life so much that he forgot what it was like to hang with his boys.

"Aye, let me get another bottle of Ace," King told the topless waitress that passed by their table.

"Nigga, you don't need shit else to drink. Ryan gone fuck yo' ass up, bruh," Rahsaan spat. He was buzzed himself and talking shit.

"Man, please. I got a stack. I'm trying to make it rain on these strippers. Get at me, bruh," King slurred.

Matter of fact, aye shorty, let me get a dance." A mocha-colored girl walked over to King and started to give him a lap dance. The dancer, who went by the name of Mocha, was doing a hell of job and King was horny. Yeah, he needed to go home to his wife.

"Let's go to the back, Daddy. I'll take care of that for you," Mocha whispered in his ear. That, along with the liquor, made his decision for him.

King got up and was headed to the Red Room with Mocha when Rahsaan stopped him.

"Aye man, what the hell you doing?"

"Man chill, I ain't about to do shit but get a private dance," King responded even though they both knew that was far from the truth. King followed Mocha to the Red Room where anything goes.

"So what can I do for you, Daddy?" Mocha asked as she bent over in King's face. He responded by pushing her head down towards his dick. All he wanted was some head. Mocha took his whole dick in her mouth and did shit he ain't never seen done. He couldn't even see his dick. It disappeared in her mouth and he wondered how the hell she got all nine inches in her mouth.

"Damn, suck that shit." King was in another world. He was so gone that he didn't realize what time it was nor did he feel his phone vibrating in his pocket, a mistake that would cost him dearly.

~ ~ ~ ~

When King stumbled in the house at 4 AM Ryan was out cold. He was so drunk that he didn't even take his clothes off; he just laid down next to Ryan. Ryan was a light sleeper and felt him when he laid down. She turned to face him but instantly backed away when she smelled the weed and alcohol on his breath. She got up so that she could help him undress.

"I hate when his ass get drunk with his friends. Got my damn bed smelling like weed and liquor," Ryan mumbled to herself. She pulled his shoes off and then his pants. When she went for his shirt she noticed what looked to be lipstick marks.

"I know this nigga didn't." She further investigated by pulling his boxers back and saw that he had lipstick marks around his dick. She instantly became enraged and hurt all mixed in one.

"King!" He didn't respond. He was snoring. She popped him upside his head.

"What the hell, Ryan?" He still didn't get up though. Ryan went to kitchen and grabbed a cup of ice water and tossed it in his face.

"Nigga, get yo' as up!" She was heated

"Man, what the fuck is yo' problem? A nigga trying to sleep and you tripping hard," he responded.

"Tripping? Nigga, who was you fucking? And before ya' ass lie the proof is right on yo' dick, nigga."

That got King's attention and his buzz was gone. He was tipsy but he now knew what was happening and he couldn't believe he had slipped and then got caught slipping. *Fuck!* The one thing he never wanted to do was hurt Ryan and he had done it.

"King, you ain't shit! I have stuck by your side through it all and this is the fucking thanks I get. I am done. This shit between us is over. I love you but I love myself more. Have a nice life." Ryan took off her wedding ring and placed it on the table. She was too drained mentally to keep up this charade with King. They had been through a lot over the past year and a half but this took the icing. She could never forgive him for this. Yeah, she knew people messed up but she never expected it from King.

"Nah Ma, I'm not about to let you just walk out on me like this. I fucked up but we're better than this." King grabbed Ryan's arm.

"Let me the fuck go!" She tried leaving again only for King to grab her and kiss her. He kissed her with so much passion that her legs went weak. It was something about this man that had a hold on her but she had to be strong. What he did was unforgettable. She pulled away from him.

"Please, King, stop. I can't do this with you." The tears were flowing and Ryan's heart was breaking in two. She had loved this man with everything in her but she didn't think she had anything left. He had literally sucked the life out of her with his mess.

King grabbed Ryan and laid her across the bed. He pulled at her pants but she pulled back. King was stronger. He took them off and snatched her thongs off. He dove head first into her wetness. Just like a man to think sex could fix things. Ryan fought against him but eventually gave in because it felt too good. Within minutes she was cumming and King savored all of her juices. She had a unique taste that he loved. He couldn't believe that he had slipped up the way he did, but shit happens and now he had to fix this.

Seeing that Ryan's body was no longer responding to him, he lifted his head up and saw her crying. He crawled up beside her and pulled her to him. He held on for dear life but it felt different. It was as if he knew that this was it for them.

"Ma, I never meant for this shit to happen. I love the hell out of you and I can't lose you." Ryan didn't respond. She was immune to the promises made by King. She was done.

One week later

King walked in the house and something felt off to him. He didn't know what, but he'd soon find out. He headed for the master bedroom to take a shower. After stripping out of his clothes he went to the closet to grab some clean clothes and that's when he felt all the air in his body leave. Ryan was gone. Her side of the closet was completely empty. He didn't have to go to the kids' rooms to see that they were empty as well. He felt it. King had lost a part of him that he probably would never get back. His rib.

Ryan had moved her and the kids to a new home. No one but Mia knew where she was. She needed some time away to sort out this mess. She loved King but his deception was unforgivable. The separation was taking a toll on her kids as well, especially Chasity who was used to King putting her to bed. She was giving Ryan a hard time. She would cry for hours until she finally cried herself to sleep. It was driving Ryan crazy but she wouldn't dare call King.

"Ry, why don't you call him and let him help you," Mia suggested. She understood what Ryan was going through being that she too went through it with Harlem.

"Nah, I'm good. I don't need him trying to slither his way back into my life. I am done with this relationship." Mia felt bad for Ryan because Ryan just found out she was pregnant and now she and King were over. She wanted to keep her baby but she was torn. She had two toddlers and a six-year-old. She couldn't do another baby right now.

"Well, let me get out of here. I have to get the kids situated for bed. Call me if you need me. Cameron, let's go," Mia called. She was taking him for the weekend and he was ready to hang with Harlem Jr." Mia and Cameron left and Ryan started dinner for the twins while they were napping. She had to get them on a schedule so that she could have time to herself. Being without King was going to be hard but she'd manage. She was a strong woman.

~ ~ ~ ~

King was sick without Ryan and it had only been one night. He tossed and turned all night. The smell of her perfume invaded his nostrils as he laid on her side of the bed. All he wanted was to turn back the hands of time and do things differently. Ryan was his heart and he could never love another like her.

He tried calling her cell phone but she'd send him right to voicemail. He missed his kids. He decided to head to his brother's house. They were known for having Cameron, especially on the weekends. After showering and getting dressed King headed out.

He was in his Audi A8 blasting Meek Mill. He rapped along with the lyrics and was feeling it.

Shorty bad as my son, is pretty in the face and no stomach/ was the city's most wanted 'til I said gimmie yo' number/ youngest nigga I'm stuntin', no more Civics from Honda/ money comin' in bundles, that's the reason she wanna lay up.

He was feeling refreshed. He knew that Ryan would eventually be back home. He wasn't going to sweat it. Until then he'd just do him.

When King pulled up to Harlem's house Cam was outside with Harlem Jr. He walked over to the two.

"What's up, son? What's up, nephew?"

"Hey, Dad." "Hey, Unc." Cameron and Harlem Jr. spoke.

"What y'all up to?" he asked as they walked towards the house.

"About to ride our bikes. Can I go home with you later, Dad?" Cameron was young but he knew his parents were going through something.

"We'll see, little man. I have to call ya' mom and ask her." Cameron was satisfied with that answer as he ran off with Harlem Jr.

"What up, sis?" King spoke as he walked in the kitchen where Mia was cooking. Unlike King, Harlem wanted no one in his kitchen but his wife, for his own reasons. Mia was a beast in the kitchen.

"I'm pissed at yo' ass right now. You know you was dead ass wrong." Mia rolled her eyes.

"I know, man. I fucked up and now my wife done left me. I need to fix this shit, sis. I'm lost without her and my kids." Mia looked at King.

"Give her time to come to grips with this. Ryan loves you but she's hurt, bro." He knew Mia was right.

"I hear you. Where my brother at?" King asked as he grabbed a bottle water from the fridge.

"Upstairs in his office." King headed up to talk to Harlem.

"What up, bro?" he spoke as he walked in the office.

"Shit, just trying to get this paperwork done. I heard yo' ass is in the dog house," Harlem joked.

"Hell yeah, I fucked up and she took my kids and left my ass." Harlem felt bad for his brother. He knew how much he loved Ryan but he couldn't intervene. They had to work this out on their own and he had faith that they would.

"Give her time, man. She'll be back eventually." That's all everyone kept saying was give her time. Fuck time, he needed his backbone back. She was the one that held him down.

"I hear what you saying man, but damn, how much time? I'm going crazy without her ass."

"She'll come around, man." King kicked it with Harlem and Mia for the remainder of the day. He was happy that at least one of his kids was there to spend time with him. How he was going to get over Ryan was beyond him.

******

King was being watched by the police. They wanted him bad but could never get any charges to stick. King was stuck between a rock and a hard place because he still had one more shipment to pick up before he was out of the game. He had to find a way to pick it up and distribute the drugs and stay off the radar at the same time. It was all too much for him to handle and he was dealing with his issues with Ryan.

"Man, you good? Harlem asked as King entered his office looking like he had the weight of the world on his shoulders. King explained what was going on and Harlem didn't have a solution just yet but he knew they would figure out something. What they didn't know was that Ryan had stopped by and heard everything when she walked by the door. She knew instantly what she had to

do. They weren't together but she'd always hold him
down.

Two weeks later....

Ryan never thought meeting Nyeem would be this
beneficial. She was one step closer to helping King. They
had the drugs and the money in place. Being that they
were using the armored truck, Ryan wasn't worried about
the police. There was no way the police were going to
pull over an armored truck. They even had the uniforms
and everything to make it seem as if they really were
guards for the armored company.

Too bad Nyeem would be disappointed in the end.
He thought he had a chance with Ryan but he didn't.
When he approached her that day in the restaurant a light
bulb went off in her head. She instantly thought of a plan
to help King. She played the situation to her advantage.
Whoever coined the phrase about pussy being power
never lied. The good part was she didn't have to give him
any. He was so stupid and naïve that he gave her what
she needed in no time.

This was supposed to be King's last shipment and
then he would be out the game for good. Knowing that he
was being watched, Ryan stepped up to handle his affairs.
She had picked up the drugs from Emilio and everything.
He was skeptical at first because she was a woman but
Ava spoke up for her. Ava was one of the most feared
women in the game. She was on some real mafia type

shit. Once Ryan got rid of these drugs and paid Emilio, King would be debt free. When it came to her King she'd go above and beyond.

"Alright ladies, let's do this shit. I'm ready to get back to my kids." Ryan got in the driver's seat and Mia in the passenger seat. Kita and Yvette were in the back with semi- automatic rifles in case shit went south. Neither lady was scared because they all had been taught by their men to shoot. They got an adrenaline rush being on this mission. They were on their way to make the drop and collect the money to pay Emilio. Ryan needed to get this over and done so that she could have a clear head.

When they pulled up to the furniture store, Mia got out with the duffle bag and went in as if she was collecting a deposit to take to the bank. The plan was fool proof. Just in case, she had a piece on her and from their time at the gun range Ryan knew Mia was nice with hers. Ryan watched the clock because Mia was only allowed to be in there for three minutes before Ryan went in for her. Being that they were expecting them, the money should have already been ready. All they had to do was switch bags with Mia. The bag they had and the one she had were identical. Just as Ryan was cocking her gun back and preparing to go in after Mia, she emerged. Mia released a breath that she didn't even know she was holding.

"Let's go," she said as she got in and Ryan pulled off.

"Damn sis, I was on my way in. I just knew those niggas tried something. Plus, Harlem would never forgive me if something had happened to you." Ryan looked over at Mia as she drove back to the warehouse in Chesterfield. She didn't look like she was scared or anything. Ryan had heard things about Mia being gangster but she had never witnessed it herself. But the cold looking chick sitting next to her was nothing like the one she chilled with on a regular basis. This was Mia, the gangstress.

"Girl, bye. I wasn't worried at all. You forgot who my husband is." They all laughed at her silly ass. It was time to finish what needed to be done.

******

When Mia walked in the house, Harlem was waiting for her. She thought she had got rid of the guard that normally followed her for safety but she didn't. A red flag went up when Mia tried to get rid of him and he alerted Harlem who made him still follow her, but from a distance. By the time he figured out what was going on it was too late. So he just tailed the girls making sure they were never in harm's way. Once they made it back to the warehouse the guard reported to Harlem what had happened. He was furious and ready to kick Mia's ass. One thing he never allowed was his woman to have any parts in this game. He wanted her as far away as possible.

"So where the hell you been?" Mia jumped at the sound of Harlem's voice. She didn't know he was up waiting for her.

"I was with Ryan. We had a late dinner and then drinks."

"Try again, damn it! You must have lost yo' damn mind!" Harlem was all up in Mia's face. He was so pissed that he was ready to put his hands on her and that was something he didn't want to do.

"First off, get out my damn face." She tried to walk away but he snatched her ass right up.

"So you a dope dealer now? Huh?"

"Nah, but my girl needed me to help her and I did. I mean, you do it, so what's the difference?"

"Are you fucking hearing yourself right now? You are a damn mother and you're out here doing drug deals."

"Look, it wasn't even like that, Harlem. Ryan called Emilio because King was in a fucked up position. They had unfinished business and because she's down for him the same way I am for you, she stepped up and did what she needed to do. I was there to help her. It was a one-time thing." Harlem couldn't believe she was justifying her wrong-doing. He understood that Ryan needed her but her kids needed her more and if she went to jail then what?

"It was stupid and anything could have happened." He didn't even wait for her to respond before he walked out. He needed to clear his head because Mia had him on ten. Mia, on the other hand, couldn't believe he was acting the way he was. They were never in any danger. She had no regrets and would do it all over again if she had to.

Chapter Nine
Lost Without You

Ryan woke up to Chasity crying. She looked over at the clock and saw that it was 3:15 AM. She had just gone to bed an hour earlier. She hadn't been able to get Chasity to sleep at all. When she finally did, it was only for an hour.

"Fuck my life." Ryan got out of the bed and headed to the twins' room to get Chasity.

"Come on, mama." Ryan took her back to her room. She was going to try a different approach. She laid down and cuddled Chasity with her but that didn't work. Ryan was ready to throw in the towel. She grabbed her cell and called King for help.

"Hello?" he answered.

"Hey King, I need your help. Chasity won't stop crying or stay asleep. She keeps saying dada dada. I haven't gotten any sleep in two days." King sat up in the bed and looked at the clock.

"Text me the address, Ma." He was tired but he'd do anything for Ryan. Plus, this was his child too and he knew why she couldn't sleep. Chasity was a daddy's girl. She always gave Ryan hell but calmed down for King. Ryan texted King her new address and threw on some sweats and a tee. After grabbing his phone and keys he headed to Southfield.

When King got to Ryan's house it was after 4 AM. He called Ryan to let her know that he was outside. When she opened the door she looked exhausted.

Damn, how long she been crying?" King asked when he heard Chasity crying.

"Since I called you." He headed upstairs where Chasity was. When he walked in she was on Ryan's bed crying and rubbing her sleepy eyes. King picked her up and she began to calm down.

"Unbelievable," Ryan stated

"Get some rest, Ma. I'll take her to the living room and get her to sleep."

"Thanks, King." Ryan got in the bed and King headed to the living room with a sleepy Chasity.

~ ~ ~ ~

When Ryan woke up it was well after 10 AM. She couldn't believe she slept that long. She got up to see if the kids were still asleep and found them in the kitchen having breakfast. She had forgot all about King coming over but was thankful.

"Good morning, Mom. Dad made us breakfast so you could sleep," Cameron offered.

"I see. Thanks, King. I really needed that sleep."

"You know I got you. I don't know why you over here doing this by ya' self anyway. We got our issues but I'm their parent too. So anything you need me to do concerning them just say it, Ma." Ryan smiled.

"Well, I'm going to go get showered and dressed since you're here with them."

"Alright. I'm gonna take Cam for a haircut today."

"Okay." Ryan headed to take her shower while King cleaned up her kitchen.

After breakfast King put the twins in their bouncers and turned on Sprout. Cameron had went to his room to play video games and King was tired.

"All I need is ten minutes," he said out loud as he laid across Ryan's bed. It felt weird as hell lying across her bed when it should have been their bed. He didn't know how much time she needed but he hoped she came home soon. He missed her like crazy. When Ryan came out of the bathroom King was laid across her bed snoring.

"I guess Daddy's little angel made him tired," she said out loud.

"I'm not sleep, Ma. Just resting my eyes. Give me five minutes and me and Cam out." She smiled as she walked out of the room. Even though they were separated her heart still fluttered for him. She was so connected with him that she couldn't stay mad at him for long, but getting back together was a no-go. She had to let King know that she wasn't going to take his shit. They could co-parent without being together.

Ten minutes later King came down with Cameron in tow.

"Alright Ma, we out. Call me if you need me." King kissed Ryan on the forehead and he and Cameron left.

"Dad, why are we in a different house then you?"

There he goes with the questions, King thought.

"Well son, sometimes grown-ups have problems that they need to work out before they can live together." King wasn't prepared for that question but he answered to the best of his ability to ease Cameron's mind.

"Well, I hope you and mommy work on your problems. I'm ready to come back home." Out of the mouths of babes. King just shook his head. He hoped they worked out their problems too. They rode in silence the rest of the way to the barbershop. When they got there Harlem was there chilling with Rahsaan.

"What up, bro?" Harlem greeted him.

"Ain't shit. Brought the lil' homey to get cut and then go to the arcade or something," King replied as he helped Cameron in the barber chair.

"I hear that, but have you and sis talked?" Harlem asked while texting on his phone.

"Nah, not yet. I did go over last night to help her with the kids and shit but that was it." At that moment King decided that he was going to get Ryan back. Whatever he needed to do he would do to have his wife back home. While Cameron got his hair cut, King sent Ryan a text.

Me: WYD Ma?

Wifey: Trying to get your daughter back to sleep. She only slept for 30 min.

Me: You need me?

Wifey: Nah, I have to get her used to just me being here.

That pissed King off. He didn't respond. Yeah, they weren't together but those were still his kids. He tried to focus on Cameron for the rest of the day. The shit with him and Ryan had him stressed to the max. Something had to give.

~ ~ ~ ~

Ryan was cooking dinner, which consisted of meatloaf, mashed potatoes, and broccoli. She had an early day tomorrow and wanted to get the kids situated early, especially Chasity. Just as she was taking the meatloaf from the oven the doorbell sounded. She assumed it was King dropping Cameron off. She headed to the door to let them in. Mia had told her about Harlem tripping on her but he still hadn't told King. Ryan didn't know how King would react, but she knew he'd find out sooner or later when he tried to get up with Emilio.

"Hey, y'all," she said, stepping aside for them to come in.

"He ate already and got his hair cut so he should be good," King said as he sat Cameron's bags down. They had gone to the arcade and then Game Stop.

"Okay, cool. Well, I'm going to feed the twins and get them ready for bed." Ryan walked away and King stared at her ass.

"Damn, she getting thick as hell," he whispered to himself before he followed her to the kitchen so that he could see the twins before he left.

He went to Christian first.

"What's up, lil' man?" As usual Chasity saw him and started trying to get out of her highchair.

"That lil' girl is a mess and it's your fault," said Ryan. King laughed.

"Well, that's my baby girl. I have to spoil her."

"Yeah well, it just makes it hard for me when you go back home." King looked at her before speaking.

"Well, if you would just bring that ass home then it would be easier for you." She rolled her eyes but didn't respond. King took that as his cue to leave. He kissed Chasity and Christian before walking towards Ryan. He bent down and kissed her on the forehead.

"See ya' later, Ma." After saying goodbye to Cameron he headed out. The longer he stayed around

Ryan the more he wanted her, and being as though she wasn't feeling him right now, it was best that he left.

~ ~ ~ ~

Surprisingly, Chasity slept through the night and Ryan was able to sleep as well. She had dropped the kids off to Mia earlier because she had a doctor's appointment.

She wasn't sure if she was keeping the baby yet but until she made her decision she had to take care of her body. She had found out that she was three months pregnant and didn't know whether or not she was going to tell King. She didn't need him trying to make her come home like he did with the twins. She took her time driving to Mia's house. She was in deep thought about the decisions she had to make. Yeah, she loved King but he had violated. Every time he was around the thought of him cheating entered her mind and that was a hard pill to swallow.

When Ryan pulled up to Mia's house King's Escalade was parked out front. She really didn't feel like him questioning why she left the twins with Mia. She would have called him but then he would have wanted to know where she was going. She was still trying to cope with the fact that she was pregnant again. She braced herself for the conversation she knew was needed.

"You gone get out the car or nah?" King had scared the shit out of her. She was in such deep thought that she didn't even notice him walk up.

"She opened the door and now stood face to face with King – well, more like face to chest because he was so much taller than her.

"Hey, King," she said as she tried to walk past him. He stood in the way blocking her.

"So where did you go that my kids couldn't go? Or better yet, why didn't you just call me to keep them? We're their parents; not Mia and Harlem." Ryan saw the vein popping out of Kings neck and knew it wasn't the time to play games with him.

"To the doctor, King. I'm pregnant." She waited for his reaction. He just stood there and looked at her for a minute before speaking.

"So what are your plans with my baby?" he asked. At that moment he didn't care that he and Ryan weren't together. She wasn't about to get rid of his seed.

"I honestly don't know, King," Ryan answered truthfully.

"Well, I know what you ain't gone do. And you can try me if you want to, Ryan," he stated before walking off. He got in his truck and pulled off. Ryan being pregnant and them living in two separate houses was too much right now.

Ryan headed in the house to get the twins and Cameron ready to go. King really didn't understand how much she was dealing with and how much she really needed him. Her pride would not allow her to tell him either.

"Hey sis, how you feel?" Mia asked Ryan as she walked in the house.

"A little fatigued but I'll manage.

"Did you tell him?" Mia asked.

"About the baby? Yes." Mia gave Ryan the side eye.

"Don't start, Mia. I'm not ready to tell him. I don't want him trying to come home out of pity. I'm dealing with enough as it is," Ryan replied as she put on Christian's shoes. Mia felt for Ryan. This was a time in her life that she needed her husband and they were at odds. She could only hope that Ryan told him soon or she'd break that promise and tell him herself. Not because she felt loyal to King, but because Ryan needed him. She was Ryan's help right now but she had her own family and couldn't always be there. Harlem was even starting to wonder what was going on because Mia had been so secretive when it came to Ryan. Ryan hadn't even told her mother.

"Ryan, think about these babies. I know you and King have your differences but whether you think so or not, honey, you need him." At that moment Ryan broke down. Mia took Christian from her and sat him on the floor. She pulled Ryan into her arms and comforted her.

"Don't worry, sis. I'm here for as long as you need me. We'll get through this."

"Will you go to chemo with me?"

Chapter Ten
In Sickness and in Health

The chemo sessions that Ryan had been taking lately were taking a toll on her body; the pregnancy only made it worse. The doctors told her that she was making progress but she didn't feel like it. Every time she bathed or dressed she saw the scar from the surgery she had two weeks ago to remove the cancerous cells. She was told by her doctor to abort the baby because of the surgery but she survived it. She felt that whatever God decided would be. She was now five months pregnant with a girl. King had been helping out more with the kids but she still hadn't told him about the cancer. She was diagnosed three months ago with stage two breast cancer. She had even begun to lose some of her hair.

Ryan sat on the porch watching the twins, who were now a year old, as they ran around. Cameron was riding his bike and just watching them brought joy to her heart. She wanted to be around to see them grow. She watched as Chasity bossed Christian around. She was the younger twin but thought she was older.

King pulled up and all the kids ran to him when he got out the car. Ryan admired the new ride he was in. He was pushing a pearl white Lexus LX. She wasn't surprised, though. King liked nice things. That was something she had grown accustomed to since meeting him. Even though they weren't together now he still paid all her bills and made sure her bank account stayed stacked.

"What's up, wife?" King greeted her with a kiss on the forehead.

"Hey, King. Nice ride, husband," Ryan replied.

"I'm glad you like it. Here." He tossed her the keys.

Damn, this nigga went out and bought me a new ride, Ryan thought as she headed to the truck to inspect it.

"This shit is fly. Thanks, husband," Ryan said as she made her way back towards him.

"Anything for you, Ma. How are you feeling?" he asked, referring to the pregnancy.

"Tired but good," Ryan smiled. She had an upcoming doctor's appointment with the oncologist. She just hoped that it would be good news because she couldn't deal with anything less.

King looked at Ryan. Something seemed off about her but he didn't know what.

"You know if you need anything, Ma, I'm here. We may not be together right now but you are still my wife and I love you," King said with much sincerity.

"I know, and I love you too, King." She really wanted to say so much more but the words didn't come out. She wanted to tell him how much she needed him but she didn't.

"So when is your next appointment?" King asked trying to change the subject. He wanted Ryan home but she obviously wasn't ready and he wasn't going to press the issue.

"Wednesday at 9 AM," Ryan responded.

"I'll be here to take you." He bent down and kissed her forehead.

"Damn, you leaving already?" Ryan didn't mean to vocally voice how she felt but it came out. King would've loved to have stayed with her but he had shit to do. Plus, until Ryan told him that she wanted him to stay, he wasn't going to. He didn't have time to play games with Ryan.

"Yeah, I got a few errands to run, but call me if you need me, Ma." Right on cue Rahsaan pulled up. He said his goodbyes to the kids and luckily Chasity didn't trip.

She was too busy telling Christian what to do. He got in with Rahsaan and they left.

When King left, Ryan felt a sense of emptiness. She needed to go home. King was her other half and she missed him like crazy. But would her pride let her go?

~ ~ ~ ~

"Mrs. Pierre, as of right now I see no signs of the cancer.

However, that doesn't mean you are in the clear. I want you to keep your appointments with me so we can monitor you and make sure that it stays gone." Ryan said a silent prayer. She was dealt a huge blow but God had a different plan. Mia was right there with her as she had been since the beginning.

The doctor left and Ryan gathered her things. She was ready to go home to her kids.

When she got home she fixed dinner and ordered a movie for her and the kids to watch. Cameron decided on Despicable Me 2 and he twins loved it. An hour after the movie started Christian was asleep. Chasity was wide awake, as usual. It was so funny to see the twins who were as different as night and day. Ryan's phone went off with a text alert. It was King.

Hubby: Open the door.

Ryan got up and headed to the door. When she opened it King was standing there looking good as hell. He was wearing black True Religions and a black and white button up. He had some black and white Pradas on his feet and his snapback was hung low, covering his eyes.

Ryan stepped to the side for him to come in but instead he pulled her to him. He had been out with his boys drinking and smoking and all he wanted to do was lay up under his wife.

"A nigga buzzed and I need to lay up under you."

He closed the door and followed Ryan to the living room where she had been watching TV with the kids.

"What up, son?" he spoke to Cameron.

"Hey, dad," he replied, never taking his eyes from the TV. Of course Chasity climbed right in his lap.

"Daddy's baby," King said as he kissed her. She got comfortable and he knew she'd be asleep in no time.

"Come over here, Ma," King told Ryan. She was sitting way on the other end of the couch. When she sat next to him he pulled her close and held her. This was what he missed the most. That night King stayed over and just held Ryan all night and she loved it so much that she didn't want him to leave the next day, but he did.

~ ~ ~ ~

Cameron was spending the weekend with King and he was ecstatic. King wasn't his biological dad but you couldn't tell Cameron that. He adored King. They were playing Xbox 360 while they waited for the pizza that King ordered.

"So what's been going on with you, son?" King always talked to Cameron one on one. He wanted to make sure he wasn't dealing with anything in school.

Cameron hesitated for a minute. He wanted to tell his dad about his mom having cancer. Ryan thought she was keeping it from everyone but Cameron knew. He had heard a conversation between Mia and Ryan.

"Well, I heard Mommy and Auntie Mia talking and Mommy is sick, dad. She thinks I don't know but I do. I try to help her a lot with the twins and around the house. I don't want her to be too tired so I do like you told me and look out for her." King couldn't believe what he was hearing. Out of the mouths of babes. He didn't know what was wrong with Ryan but if his son was concerned then he would check it out.

"Well, no worries, son. I'll take care of it, okay?"
Cameron shook his head. They continued their night and
King told himself that he was going to check on Ryan the
next day when he picked her up for her doctor's
appointment.

The next day King and Cameron headed to Ryan's
house so he could take her to the doctor. King let himself
in. He had a key because he paid the bills. Ryan didn't
agree with him being able to come and go as he pleased
but she didn't have a choice messing with King. He found
Ryan upstairs getting the twins dressed for the day.
Consuela had been coming to Ryan's to help out with the
kids.

"What's up, wife?" King spoke as he walked in the
room.

"Hey," Ryan said. She was extremely tired and had
no energy. That was one of the issues she experienced
with cancer. She had her good days and then there were
days she felt bad.

"Daddy!" Chasity was trying to get away from
Ryan to get to King. He walked over and picked her up.

"Hey, Daddy's baby." He kissed her and she laid her
head on his shoulder. Ryan shook her head at how

spoiled Chasity was. She put on Christian's shoes and he ran out the room.

"You ready to go Ma?" King studied Ryan. She didn't look sick at all. In fact she looked damn good to be five months pregnant.

"Yeah, I'm ready." They headed out the door giving Chasity to Consuela on the way.

~ ~ ~ ~

"What the hell is that?" King pointed to the scar by Ryan's right breast. She was speechless. She had forgotten all about the scar but was busted. King had a look on his face that said he wasn't playing games with her.

"It's a scar from surgery," she said in a low voice.

"Come again." King wasn't sure he heard her right. She repeated herself.

"Surgery from what, Ryan? And why the hell didn't your husband know?"

"King, I was diagnosed with breast cancer when I was two months pregnant. I didn't know I was pregnant at the time but we were going through our issues and I was torn between keeping my baby and going through with the surgery. I just didn't want you to feel sorry for me. I wanted us to get back right on our own, not because I was sick." King was furious. He couldn't believe Ryan had kept something like that from him. His son was right about her being sick.

"You know what, I am at a loss for words right now. I mean, that's something that I should have known because it doesn't just affect you. This was some selfish shit you did." King walked out of the exam room and headed to the car. He couldn't even look at Ryan at that point. Anything could have happened to her and she didn't even tell him. She was sick while she looked after his kids. He didn't know if she was still sick but he feared losing her. Right then King did something he couldn't ever remember doing; he prayed. He prayed for the strength to deal with this and the strength to bring his family back together.

Ryan got dressed and headed outside to the car. She didn't know what state King was in but she had kept her secret from him and couldn't be mad at him for being upset. She just hoped he was able to forgive her. When she got to the car King was sitting there in deep thought.

"King, look, I'm sorry. I know that it doesn't change the fact that I didn't tell you but I'm sorry." She touched his arm. He looked at her.

"It's cool, Ma." She was surprised at his response. King was such a hot head and he never forgave that easily. They rode home in silence. Ryan didn't say anything because she didn't know what type of mood King was in. She just hoped that he would forgive her for keeping her sickness a secret.

King pulled up to Ryan's house and she got out.

"I'll be back later, Ma. Call me if you need me," he said before she made it to the door. He had to clear his head. His wife needed him but never told him. He felt like shit because had he not fucked up he would have been there for her. If something was to happen to Ryan he'd never forgive himself. He headed to Harlem and Mia's house; she was the one person that would give it to him straight, no chaser. He needed her opinion on what to do.

Chapter Eleven
I'll Always Love You

King had been at Ryan's house every day since her appointment last week. He didn't sleep there but he was there in the morning and at night he tucked the kids in. He made sure that Ryan didn't lift a finger. As much as she hated not doing anything, she loved the fact that King was there. She didn't know if it was just her hormones or if she genuinely missed his touch but she was horny as ever and King was looking good.

"Alright Ma, the twins are sleep and Cam is in the bed. I'll see y'all tomorrow." It was well after 9 PM and King was headed home to sleep alone, as he had been for the past three months.

"It's late. You can stay if you want." Ryan was in the bed watching TV.

"Nah, Ma. As much as I would love to stay I don't want to confuse my son. If we're gonna sleep under the same roof then it's gonna be because we're back together, as husband and wife in every aspect." With that he walked out leaving Ryan's mouth open. That night Ryan tossed and turned. All she wanted was her husband back but her pride wouldn't let her tell him.

~ ~ ~ ~

Harlem and Mia were having a cookout and everyone was there. Kita and Markie, Tez and Yvette, Ryan and all the kids. Harlem's mom and King's mom were there as well. The only person that hadn't showed up yet was King. Mia noticed Ryan looking for King and she went over to talk to her.

"Hey sis, you good?" Mia and Ryan had become really close. You could say they were best friends. Mia had been there for her in more ways than one. She had took time away from her own family to tend to Ryan when she was sick.

"Yeah, I'm not gone lie, though; I was hoping King came. Mia, I miss him and I'm ready to go back home." That made Mia smile. She knew how much King loved Ryan and vice versa. They were going through a rough patch in their relationship but hey were made for each other.

"I'm sure he'll be here," Mia replied before walking away. Ryan decided to text him to see if he was coming over.

Me: Hey r u coming to the cookout?

A few minutes later she got a text back:

Hubby: No he's not. He's busy

"What the hell?" Ryan said out loud.

Me: Who the hell is this?
Hubby: None of your business, now stop texting my man.

Ryan was pissed. She knew they weren't together but she still felt some type of way. He was still her husband but it seemed as if she took too long to let go of what he did because he had obviously moved on. Her heart broke in two. She never pictured the day that she and King would be over. She was ready to go home. She couldn't take being around all the couples. With her mom keeping the kids with her for the weekend she'd be able to have time to herself. She bid everyone goodbye and headed home.

King was sitting in his office at the Pink Kitty doing truck orders for the liquor and food. He looked at the time and saw that he was late for the cookout. He decided to call Harlem and let him know he would be there later when he realized his phone was gone. He remembered he was by the bar earlier so it should've been there. They weren't open yet so nobody could have taken it.

"Aye Toya, did I leave my phone down here?" he asked the bar maid. She smiled and passed him his phone. He took it from her and headed back to his office to finish up.

Five minutes later Toya walked in. She had always been attracted to King. He was a very prominent man with money and he was fine.

"Hey Toya, what can I do for you?" King asked, looking up from his paperwork. She didn't speak but instead walked over to him and straddled his lap. King was caught off guard.

"Whoa, what are you doing?" He tried to push her off of him.

"Please, King. I see the way you look at me. Hell, you're a single man now and we're both grown."

126

"Nah Ma, I'm a married man who loves his wife. So I need for you to get out my office and if I was you I'd never mention this again or you'll be looking for a new job. He pushed her all the way off him. Yeah, any man with eyes could see that Toya was bad but King had hopes of reconciling with his wife; the only woman he ever loved. Once Toya left he decided it was time to go. He would just work from home. He gathered his things and left.

Ryan decided to go to the house she used to share with King. She didn't know if he had company but she didn't care. It was time for her to claim what belonged to her. When she got there King's car wasn't there so she assumed he was at the woman's house. She'd just wait for him to get home. When she walked in the house everything was the same as she had left it. She had missed this house. Ryan made her way up the stairs to the master bedroom and climbed in the bed. She was extremely tired from crying her eyes out. Almost as soon as she hit the pillow she was out.

When King pulled up to his home in Bellville he was surprised to see Ryan's car there but excited at the same time. He didn't know what this meant but he was happy. He headed in the house and found Ryan asleep in the master bedroom.

"Damn, she finally brought her ass home." King said a silent prayer, thanking god for bringing Ryan back. He stripped down to his boxers and climbed in bed next to his wife. He pulled Ryan close to him and she stirred.

"Welcome home, Ma."

When King woke up the next day Ryan's side was empty. He thought maybe he was dreaming last until he saw her walk out of the bathroom.

"Morning, wife," he said as he watched her move around the bedroom.

"Morning," she replied. Yeah, she was happy to be home but what about the chick King was seeing? She decided to address the issue before they went any further.

"So whoever the chick was that texted me from your phone yesterday, dead it. Tell that bitch wifey is home." King was confused because he wasn't seeing anyone. Then it dawned on him what she was talking about. *That bitch,* he thought.

"Nah Ma, ain't nobody else. But I know who had my phone and that broad is as good as fired. No worries, Ma." Ryan didn't even question what he was talking about; as long as it was handled. Ryan was feeling tired so she got back in bed and cuddled under King.

"Are you okay, Ma?" King was worried about

Ryan. He didn't know much about breast cancer but he had started researching it and he planned to go to her appointments with the oncologist from here on out.

"Yeah, I'm just tired." King just laid there holding her. What God has joined together let no man put asunder. They were made for each other and would always have a connection.

Ryan still thought King had no idea of what she and the girls did, but he knew. It was just an argument he didn't want to have with her right now. However, he did let Emilio know not to ever deal with her or Mia again business-wise. The next time, he wasn't going to be so forgiving.

Chapter Twelve
A Turn for the Worst

Ryan hadn't been in the best of spirits. The cancer was back and she was weaker than ever. She couldn't even make it to the bathroom by herself. She couldn't hold her bowels and she hated that King saw her like this but he didn't care. Their wedding vows said for better or worse and he was by her side through it all.

"Come on Ma, let's get you back in the bed." King helped Ryan back to bed. She was now seven months pregnant but didn't look like it due to the extreme weight loss. She had lost most of her hair and felt ugly even though King reminded her every day that she was beautiful.

"I want to see my babies." Ryan didn't know what was going to happen with this cancer thing but she wanted to spend as much time as possible with her kids and husband because tomorrow wasn't promised.

"Okay, I'll go get them. Just relax, okay Ma?" She shook her head as King headed out the door. He came back a few minutes later with the twins and Cameron in tow.

"Hey, Ma. How are you feeling?" Cameron was so wise beyond his age. He was the man of the house when his dad wasn't home. He made sure Ryan didn't need anything and was a great big brother to the twins.

"I'm feeling okay, baby. I just wanted to spend some time with you guys." Ryan forced a weak smile. King had been in contact with a few cancer treatment centers. He needed the best care for his wife. He had to assure that she'd be here to raise their kids. It seemed as though she was wasting away right before him.

After spending a little time with the kids, King wanted Ryan to rest. He had Consuela look after the kids while he sat with Ryan.

"Do you need anything, Ma?" King asked.

"No, I just wanna rest." Ryan closed her eyes and was soon asleep.

~ ~ ~ ~

"King! Oh my God I'm bleeding and it's everywhere!" Ryan was frantic as King woke up and saw all the blood everywhere. He didn't know where she was bleeding from but the bed was soaked. He called 911 and they were there within five minutes. King was scared because he thought he was losing his wife. Once they had Ryan on the gurney she was transported to the hospital with King right by her side. The whole ride she kept losing consciousness and that scared King.

Once they got there Ryan was wheeled back and King had to stay back. King was waiting in the waiting room when Harlem and the rest of their family and friends came. Mia was the first to be by King's side.

"It's going to be okay, bro. She's a strong woman and she has a lot to live for." King forced a smile.

"Thanks, sis." He really wasn't up for talking so nothing else was said.

The doctor came out an hour later.

"Mr. Pierre, can I speak with you for a minute?" King, along with Mia, walked over with the doctor.

"We had to perform an emergency C-section and she didn't survive. I'm sorry. We can make preparations for the body whenever you're ready.

~ ~ ~ ~

This was hard for King. He loved his family with everything in him but to bury one of them was hard. He spared no expense for his baby girl. She had to go out right.

"Are you okay?" Mia asked as they stood at the burial site. There wasn't a dry eye around. She was so young and hadn't even begun to live.

"Yeah, I'm good," King smiled as he looked at his wife. He knew this was hard for her because she had felt their baby move inside her and had seen her born. Now she was their angel in Heaven. They had named her Angel Love Pierre.

"Let's go, Ma. She's resting in peace now." That day at the hospital Ryan went into early labor and Angel didn't make it. The umbilical cord was wrapped around her neck and she was stillborn. Ryan's body was too weak to carry her and it took a toll on her as well.

They headed back home to celebrate the home going of Angel.

Three months later

Ryan had been doing a lot better and her cancer was in remission. She was still trying to cope with the loss of Angel. She was on birth control because she feared losing another baby. King had been her support through it all and she loved him more for it. Today they were going out for the first time since being back together. Mia and Harlem, as well as Kita, Markie, Tez, and Yvette were also joining them.

They were hitting up Club Skyy and Ryan was looking fierce. They were straight stunting on hos. Ryan was rocking a pink crocheted lace crop top with a pair of bleached denim shorts. Her shoe game was sick. She rocked a pair of black Monolo Blahnik peep-toe boots. Her hair had grown back so she was rocking a head wrap. King, being that nigga, had her iced out. She was outshining him and that's the way he liked it.

When they walked in Club Skyy all eyes were on them. Everyone knew who King and Harlem were. The chicks were thirsty but neither Mia nor Ryan gave a damn. They knew their positions. Once they got to VIP they kicked off the night with a bottle of Ace of Spades and a bottle of Remy Martin. King sat back while Ryan danced for him. He was getting his own little private show in the corner. When Beyoncé's "Rocket" came on, she turned it up a notch. She moved seductively and King was stuck.

Let me sit this ass on you/ Show you how I feel/ Let me take this off / Will you watch me?

Her body was flawless and the faces she made had him ready to bend her over right then and there. She sat on his lap and started to grind as Beyoncé's words blared through the speakers. King was in love all over again. He had a bad bitch and she was all his.

Don't take your eyes off it/ Watch it, babe/ If you like you can touch it, baby/ Do you, do you wanna touch it, baby?

King grabbed her waist and held her in place while he whispered in her ear. "You know I'ma fuck the shit out of you, right?" Ryan just smiled as she tried to get up. King grabbed her. "Nah Ma, you not about to get up while my dick is hard. I don't need nobody seeing that shit."

"No worries, Daddy. I got you later." Before he could respond Toya walked up with two other girls.

"What's up, King?" He waved but never took his off Ryan.

"Damn, you that caught up in wifey that you cant't speak?" Toya continued

"Look bitch, he spoke. Now beat ya' feet and stop trying to get attention." Ryan was annoyed. She saw how Toya always looked at King but she wasn't about to be disrespected.

"Damn Ry, it ain't that serious, Ma," Toya laughed as she walked away.

"Bitch!" Ryan tried to jump up but King grabbed her.

"Chill, Ma. She ain't worth it." Ryan gave King the evil look.

"Let me find out."

"Find out what? Man, go'n with that shit, Ma. We was having a good time so chill." Ryan didn't know what was up with Toya, but she didn't like her and was ready to whoop her ass.

Toya watched King and Ryan from the dance floor. She hated Ryan because she had everything she wanted. The man, the kids, and the house. She vowed to take Ryan's spot as King's main bitch. The one thing King didn't know was that Ryan and Toya were half-sisters. Ryan didn't even know but Toya would hold on to that information until it was needed.

"Why the fuck is that bitch looking over here?" Mia caught the incident between Ryan and Toya and had been watching Toya since. Harlem knew Mia and didn't want her popping off so he tried to take control of the situation.

"Chill, Ma. Let it go." She did, for now. But trust, she was ready if needed.

Young Jeezy's "Lose My Mind" came on and the girls headed to the floor. King was happy to see Ryan enjoying life again. He still had to take care of Imran and Tish and now it seemed as if Toya was going to be a problem. He was ready to go home and cuddle with his wife but he wanted her to enjoy herself.

He sat back and lit his blunt. Things had definitely come full circle for him. All he had to do was take care of the problems that had caused his family turmoil and things would be A-1.

Chapter Thirteen
Gangstress

Something was telling King not to trust Toya so he had some info dug up on her and what he found threw him for a loop. He didn't tell anyone about the info he received just yet; especially not Ryan. He wanted to confront Toya first. He had a few RBM members pay Imran a visit and he was no longer a factor. Tish, on the other hand, had disappeared. King wasn't worried because if he knew Tish, she'd show up sooner or later and he'd be ready for her.

Little did King know while he was looking for Tish, his wife was laying down her gangster.

******

"So you thought you could take over my life? Bitch, you're funny. See, you could never be me because I'm a boss bitch and I'm married to a boss. But what you did pissed me off. I don't play about my man or my kids and you violated both, so now I have to violate you. I don't know why you hos keep trying me. King will never leave me and you will never be me." Ryan drew back and punched Tish in the face.

"Argh!" Tish spit out blood and laughed. "That's all you got?" she taunted Ryan.

"Shut up, bitch, and take this ass whooping," Ryan retorted. She was tired of people coming between her and King's relationship. Mia just sat and watched Ryan. There was no need for Mia to step in because Ryan could hold her own.

"These broads will never learn," Mia said out loud. She sat and watched as Ryan handled her business. She knew King would be mad but he'd eventually get over it. Ryan had to let this broad know who was wifey.

While King was doing his investigations, Ryan was doing her own. She found out that Tish was working with Imran. She felt stupid because she fell right into Tish's trap. They had played her but now it was her turn to have fun. She'd explain to King later. Of course she was prepared for his reaction; especially knowing King, but he could never understand how she felt. This was his ex bitch being manipulative and Ryan needed to let her know who the queen was.

Mia watched Ryan pull out a nine millimeter and was a little shocked. She was far from scared but didn't know that they were committing a murder. She thought they were there to rough Tish up, but it seemed as if Ryan had other plans. Ryan stuck the gun in Tish's face.

"Open ya mouth, bitch! Now give me one good reason why I shouldn't kill you." Tish laughed which further pissed Ryan off. She wasn't a weak bitch and she was about to prove her point. Before anyone knew what had happened, Ryan pulled the trigger and Tish's brain matter was everywhere.

"Well done, sis. Even though we didn't come here for that you handled yours. Now we have to make that call to clean this mess up." Mia knew Harlem would flip so she called one of the baddest bitches on the West Coast; Ava Williams.

Ava was Harlem's and King's older sister but she was also a boss in the game. She had much clout and niggas and bitches feared her.

"Ava, I need a clean-up crew in. My carpet got real dirty, Ma," Mia spoke in the phone."

"You still live in the same spot, sis?" Ava asked, referring to the warehouse that Harlem did his dirt in.

"Yup." With that Mia ended the call. She knew Ava would take care of it.

"Let's go, Ma." They headed out and went home to their families.

******

"So why did you come here? You knew all along that Ryan was your sister," King confronted Toya. They were in his office at The Pink Kitty.

"Yeah, and?" She was real nonchalant about the situation.

"Look, I don't know what you want from her but you're barking up the wrong tree. I don't play with my family and I won't hesitate to put a hot one in you." Toya laughed as she walked over to King. She reached for his dick and he smacked her hands away.

"Bitch, is you stupid?" Toya wanted King. In fact she wanted to take Ryan's place, period. She was on some real life *Fatal Attraction* shit. She had been riding past their home and even peeping in their bedroom while they had sex. She was turned on to the fullest and wouldn't stop until she got Ryan's life.

"You know you want this pussy, King, and I'm willing to give it to you, but Ryan is coming between us and I won't stand for it." With that she walked out, leaving King speechless.

He knew he had to do something about her because she was going to cause problems.

Chapter Fourteen
You Thought I was Gone

Ryan had just gotten the twins to sleep and
Cameron was in his room. All she wanted was a shower
and sleep. She had sent Consuela home for the night and
King hadn't come home yet. Ryan grabbed her iPod and
put it on the dock. When she got the water just right she
got in and instantly she felt relaxed.

"Get the fuck out the shower, bitch!" Ryan damn
near slipped in the tub. She had forgotten all about
Prince. Fuck, how did she get caught slipping? She
wasn't moving fast enough for him so he snatched her out
the shower by her hair.

"Argh!" Ryan yelled out in pain.

"Shut up, bitch!" he pushed her in the room and
she fell on the bed.

"Why are you doing this, Prince?" Ryan asked.
All she could think about was her babies. She hoped that
King was on his way home because she really needed
him right now.

"You were supposed to be my bitch but you
playing house with this nigga," Prince spewed.

"Prince, we are over. I am back with my
husband." That comment pissed him off. He drew back
and punched her in the face. The punch was so powerful
that she was sure her jaw was broken. Ryan couldn't

believe this was happening. It was like she wasn't meant
to be happy. She was convinced that she was cursed.

Cameron had heard the commotion and he knew
his dad wasn't home. He took his siblings and hid in the
closet with the phone. After making sure they were calm,
he called his dad and told him that something wasn't
right. Cameron was a pretty smart child and knew that
this was an emergency. Never once did he panic; King
had taught him well. King kept him on the phone the
whole time. He called Harlem and Rahsaan to meet him
at the house.

The usual fifteen minutes it took him to get home
from the club took less than ten. He had his twin nine
millimeters ready. He entered the house from the back
right along with Harlem and Rahsaan. They could hear
the commotion going on upstairs as they made their way
up slowly and quietly. The door to the master bedroom
was slightly ajar and King could see Prince standing over
Ryan about to commit a sexual assault. His eyes
connected with Ryan's and he put his finger to his lips
signaling her to be quiet. He wanted to catch Prince off
guard. Prince was so caught up with trying to sample
Ryan's goods that he had sat his gun down, leaving him
without a weapon. King crept up on him and slammed his
gun into the back of his head. He could have just shot
him but he wanted him to see who was sending him to his
maker.

"So you thought you could just come up in my
house and fuck with my wife, nigga?" King hit him again
with the gun.

"Fuck you, nigga!" Prince shouted.

"You talking shit and your life is about to end, bitch!" King didn't even give him a chance to respond. He put two in his dome.

"I'll call the clean-up crew. You get Ryan and the kids and go to my house," Harlem replied. King went to Ryan and examined her face.
"Damn, Ma. I should have been here." King felt like shit for not being there to protect his family. He didn't feel bad about the security guards that were watching over his home. Somehow Prince was able to take them all out and that was unacceptable. He hired them to protect his home and they failed. "Here Ma, put this on. I'm gonna go get the kids ready to go." King passed her a jogging suit to put on while he went downstairs to get the kids. When he opened the closet door Cameron was still there with his siblings who were asleep.

"You did good, son." That night they stayed at Harlem's while their place was cleaned. However, King started looking for a new house. He wanted a fresh start with his family. So much had happened in that house and it was time to move on.

Chapter Fifteen
New Beginnings

King had found a new home in Southfield. It had five bedrooms and three baths. It wasn't as big as their old home but it was big enough. He just wanted Ryan to feel comfortable.

"So you like it, Ma?" She smiled because she couldn't talk. Her jaw had been wired shut due to the beating she endured from Prince. King wanted to shed a tear every time he saw her. He still blamed himself for not being there.

Ryan had been getting mysterious phone calls. When she would answer the person would hang up and then call right back. It was starting to get on her nerves. She was finally able to talk again and was ready to curse somebody out. She turned her cell off because she was irritated. She looked over at her husband and smiled. They had really been through a storm but they had survived. Every day he showed her how much he loved her and she was thankful for him.

Ryan was horny and ready to play. She went under the cover and grabbed King's erect dick. *"What the hell is he dreaming about?* She thought, wondering why his dick was already hard and he was asleep.

"Yeah, that's what happens when I sleep next to my sexy ass wife." Ryan smiled.

"No fair. You were playing sleep," she pouted.

"I wasn't playing sleep. You assumed I was sleep. Now come here." He pulled her to him and kissed her lips. She straddled his lap and just as he pulled her breasts out, in came Chasity. Ryan huffed her breath. She loved her kids but that Chasity was always blocking. King laughed at Ryan.

"We'll finish later, Ma." Chasity went right to her dad.

"I guess I'm going to get breakfast started." They no longer used the chef because Ryan wanted to cook. However, they did keep Consuela to help with the kids. King wanted Ryan to be able to relax sometimes.

Ryan headed to the kitchen. She saw the mailman leave the porch so she checked the mail. It was a bunch of bills and then a blank envelope. It wasn't addressed to anyone so she opened it. It was pictures of her, the kids, and King.

"King!" she yelled. Just when they thought everything was going good someone always tried to fuck with them. King came down with Chasity in his arms.

"What's wrong, Ma?" he asked, concerned. She passed him the envelope.

"Where did you get these?" He was pissed. Somebody was still trying him.

"From the mailbox. I don't like this shit, King," Ryan said as she took eggs from the fridge.

"Don't worry, Ma. I'll take care of it." King put his daughter down and headed upstairs. He needed somebody on this right away. He needed to know who was watching his family. He wasn't about to let shit get out of hand again.

George Carter sat in front of the parole board awaiting their decision. He had pleaded his case on being reformed and explained that he could function in society if they release him. He had been in and out of jail for the last eleven years. He initially went for child molestation and then for possession of a controlled substance.

"Mr. Carter, we have reviewed your case and decided to grant you a release under the condition that you stay in a halfway house for the first sixty days. During that time you are to seek employment and attend counseling sessions for sex offenders. You are not to be around any minors nor are you to be anywhere near a school. Is that understood, Mr. Carter?" Carter was happy.

"Yes, ma'am." He wanted to jump for joy. All that was on his mind was finding his daughter Ryan. He had an infatuation with her and dreamt about her often. He knew she was a full grown woman now and that made is dick jump. Yeah, to some he was sick but to him he was just a man. He was so wrapped up in what he was going to do once he was released that he didn't hear anything else that was said to him. Little did he know it wouldn't be easy to get Ryan. King made sure she was well-protected because of the past mishaps.

Ryan was getting ready for a cookout at Harlem and Mia's house. She had just got the twins ready and Cameron was already over there. All she had to do now was get dressed. She was looking forward to chilling with her girls. They had all became one big family and Ryan loved it. Before meeting King all she had was her mom and Cameron.

"You ready, Ma?" King asked as he walked in the room.

"Almost," she said as she slipped on her shoes.

"Did you remember the juice for the kids?" Ryan asked King as she applied her lip gloss.

"Yeah, everything is already in the car. I'm just waiting on yo' slow self." Ryan rolled her eyes.

"Whatever, punk." She threw a pillow at him. They headed out the door to go chill and enjoy the family.

Chapter Sixteen
A Family Affair

Everyone was enjoying themselves. They had the old school jams playing, the grill going, and the kids running around. The guys had a game of spades going and the grandparents were under the tree for shade. It was definitely a family affair.

"Nigga, that's our book!" Harlem shouted at Tez.

"Nah homey, yo' ass reneged!" Tez shouted back.

"When?" Harlem hated losing at spades. It was always a competitive game when it came to the guys. The women stayed out of it.

Mia wanted to have a girl's weekend in Miami. She thought it would be nice. The thing was talking Harlem into letting her go. He was so overprotective that he barely wanted her out of his sight.

"So ladies, what do y'all think about a trip to Miami?" Mia asked when they were away from the men.

"Hell yeah!" Kita replied. "That shit would be dope."

"I'm definitely down," Yvette replied.

"You already know I'm going. I could use the break," Ryan replied.

That settled it. They were headed to Miami in two weeks. Now all they had to do was get their men to agree.

~ ~ ~ ~

The women were out shopping for their Miami trip. They balled out without even looking at tags. That's what happened when you were a hustler's wife. Ryan bought four new swimsuits, new shorts and shirts, as well as five new pair of shoes. She didn't overdo it because she knew they'd be in Miami shopping as well.

"Damn, we ready or nah?" Kita joked about all the bags they had.

"Shit, I know I am. Now let's go back to my house and sip something," Mia offered. They left the mall and headed to Mia's house.

When they got there the guys were in the basement playing pool and smoking. Ryan and Mia decided to cook food for everyone. They were kid-free for the whole weekend. Harlem's mom and King's mom had them all. Thank God for grandparents.

"So what are we cooking?" Ryan asked.

"Let's keep it simple and do fried chicken, mashed potatoes, and a salad."

"Sounds good to me." The ladies prepared dinner and talked shit.

"Damn, this wine is good as hell. I need another glass," Kita said as she downed her glass.

"No, you don't," Markie said coming up the stairs.

"Take ya' ass back downstairs, bruh. We chilling up here." Markie smacked her on the ass.

"What y'all cooking? A nigga hungry," Harlem asked as he made his way into the kitchen along with the other men.

"Chicken, mashed potatoes, and a salad. It's actually about ready so get settled and we'll bring everything to the dining room," Mia replied as she strained the last batch of chicken. The men made their way into the dining room and the women brought all the food in. They ate, joked, and just had a good time. It felt good to have a conversation about something other than cartoons and video games.

Chapter Seventeen
I'm in Miami, Bitch!

The girls had got the guys to let them go, surprisingly without a fight. Mia thought they had something up their sleeves because there was no way they'd let them go without an argument, but she wasn't going to worry about it. Right now she was on vacation with her girls.

"Let's go to the beach. I wanna show off this new bikini," Kita shouted from the bathroom. They were all in Kita's room chilling.

"Okay, bitch, you gone have Markie beat that ass," Mia joked.

"Girl please, ain't nobody worried. I know where home is. I just wanna go have fun," Kita replied as she peeked out the bathroom.

"Whatever. I'm down," Ryan chimed in.

"I'll pass. I want to go to the spa," Mia replied and Yvette offered to go with her.

So Ryan and Kita went to the beach and Mia and Yvette headed to the spa, all making plans to meet up for dinner later.

"Damn, it's hot as hell but I'm loving it out here," Ryan said. She pulled her towel out and laid it on the sand. She was clad in an all black Chanel swimsuit. It was a bad piece too. The top was separated from the bottom only joined together by strings and had a diamond in the middle.

Kita had on a simple Louis Vuitton two-piece, but both girls were looking fly.

"Damn, lil' mama, you looking nice." Ryan jumped up.

"What the hell are you doing here, King?" she asked jumping in his arms.

"Oh y'all thought we was gone let y'all come to Miami without us? Nah, not gone happen, Ma," he replied, looking at her like she was the main course.

"Whatever," she replied.

"You look nice in this piece, Ma," he said as he brought her close to him. Markie was over in the water with Kita. They chilled at the beach until it was time to meet for dinner. They had decided on Scarpetta, an Italian restaurant in Miami Beach.

Ryan and King were getting dressed for dinner, and when King saw what she had on he wanted her right then and there. She had on a strapless white Gucci jersey dress and a pair of black and gold Balenciaga pumps.

"Damn Ma, you looking good as hell." King knew he had a bad bitch and he kept her dressed in the finest. He went to his suitcase to retrieve a gift he had bought for her just because.

"Here, Ma." She smiled as she opened the jewelry box. It was a pair of two-carat princess cut diamond studs.

"Babe, these are the bomb. Thanks!" She took off the earrings that she had originally put on and replaced them with the new pair. King loved to spoil her and she loved it.

"Now let's go before we don't make it to dinner." They laughed as they made their way out.

~ ~ ~ ~

They had partied the whole week in Miami. It was their last night there and they were headed to the Skybar to have drinks.

"This trip was nice. I enjoyed it so far," Ryan said as they were pulling up.

"Yeah, it was nice. I'll have to take you away more often," King replied, putting his hand on her knee.

"I do miss my kids, though," she commented. They pulled in the valet area and got out. King grabbed Ryan's hand and they met the rest of the crew in their reserved area.

"So what can I get for you guys tonight?" the waitress asked.

"I'll have an Amaretto Sour," Ryan gave her drink order.

"You can send over a bottle of Remy as well," Harlem replied. After everyone's drink orders were placed they chatted about their trip.

"We definitely have to do this again," Mia said.

"I agree. We had so much fun," Kita commented. Before anyone could respond someone walked up to their table.

"Damn Harlem, it's been too long! Good to see you." He didn't recognize the woman so he just threw his hands up in a nonchalant greeting. Mia looked at him.

"Don't start, Ma. I don't even know who that is," he whispered in her ear. The woman was still standing there.

Uh, can I help you with something?" Mia asked.

"You can't, but he can," she said, pointing at Harlem.

"Look bitch, beat it," Kita started.

"Well if you want to get at me again, Harlem, you know where to find me. You know, once you get rid of ya' groupies." Mia had heard enough. She tossed her drink in the girl's face and before anyone knew what had happened, she was beating her ass. Harlem pulled Mia off the girl but that only made her swing on him.

"You fucking with these bitches again, Harlem? I told you not to fuck with me." *Pop!* She swung again. He caught her arms this time.

"Mia, chill the fuck out. I told you I didn't even know who the fuck that bitch was!"
He really didn't know who she was. It could have been some chick he boned a long time ago. Since he and Mia got back together he hadn't messed with anyone else. He had learned his lesson.

156

"Nigga, you got me fucked up if you think I believe that shit. The bitch knew you. I'm sick of this shit. If you gone cheat then a least keep that shit away from me, nigga." Mia walked off and Kita followed. Everybody was in shock at what went down. Mia and Harlem were the ideal couple so to see them into it was major.

"Damn bro, who was that bitch?" King asked.

"Man, I honestly don't know. This shit is not happening right now." Harlem got up and walked out in search of Mia. King dropped a hundred dollar bill on the table and everyone else followed suit. By the time they got outside Mia was getting in a cab with Kita. Kita called Markie to let him know she was with Mia. She didn't want her to be alone traveling around Miami.

Harlem headed back to the hotel to wait for her but she never showed up. He called her cell numerous times but only got her voicemail. Mia had sent Kita back to the hotel around midnight and she caught a redeye flight home. She didn't want to be anywhere near Harlem.

******

They were at the airport and no one wanted to board the plane without Mia. They thought she was still in Miami. Kita tried calling her again. This time she answered.

"Yeah, Kita?" She sounded as if she had been crying.

"Where you at, mama? We at the airport waiting on you," Kita spoke into the phone.

"Go ahead and board the plane, ma. I caught a redeye last night. I'm home with my kids." Kita breathed a sigh of relief.

"Okay mama, see you in a little while." She hung up and turned to Harlem.

"She's already home." They proceeded to the departure gates. This was about to be a long flight. All the women were mad at Harlem and the men were mad because their wives were mad.

"Man, if I don't get no pussy 'cause you fucked up, I'm kicking yo' ass, nigga," King whispered in Harlem's ear.

"Man, get the fuck on." He wasn't in the mood for no jokes. He had to make shit right with his wife.

Chapter Eighteen
Payback's a Bitch

Mia had been sleeping in the guest room and Harlem was walking around like a sad puppy. He didn't know how this shit had happened or who this chick was. He had to figure out a way to fix this. He had went out and bought her a few gifts. He didn't know if it would help but it was worth a try. He sat the three boxes on the bed in the guest room and headed out. He was meeting up with the guys to play basketball. When he pulled up to the court the guys were already there.

"Harlem, my man, what's good?" Markie said giving him dap.

"Ain't shit. Still trying to get back in good with the wife." He took his towel out of his gym bag and wiped the sweat from his forehead.

"Damn, bruh, that was two weeks ago. She ain't over it yet?" King responded.

"Hell nah. Mia ass is known for holding grudges. I just wish it was for something I had actually done."

"I hear that," Markie replied.

"Well, let's get this game going," Tez added as he tossed the ball to King. They played ball for a good two hours before calling it day.

When Harlem got home Mia was there and dinner was done. That was one thing about her; they might have been beefed out but she still took care of home. She was in the family room with the kids watching TV when he walked in.

"Hey, Dad," Harley spoke." She was truly a daddy's girl. She had Harlem wrapped around her fingers. He never told her no.

"What's up, lil' mama?" he asked, sitting next to her." Mia ignored him but he was done playing games with her. He stood up and pulled Mia with him. He pulled her in the kitchen.

"Look Ma, I don't know who that chick was in Miami. It could have been a chick from a long time ago. I have not cheated on you since we've been married. I have learned my lesson and all this silent treatment shit, dead it. Move ya' shit back in the room and start acting like my wife." With that being said Harlem headed upstairs to shower. He wasn't dealing with this shit from Mia again. She had to learn not to let someone else tell her about her husband. She had to trust him. Harlem wasn't worried because he knew that he and Mia had an unbreakable bond and would always find their way back to each other.

~ ~ ~ ~

Mia still didn't believe Harlem. She didn't know why but her woman's intuition was telling her different. Tonight she was stepping out. She needed some "me time." She headed to Club Skyy. She didn't wait in line because the bouncer was flirting with her. She gave him a false name and number before going inside the club. She hadn't been out since Miami and the atmosphere was pretty nice.

"Excuse me, sweetie. I was wondering if I could have a moment of your time?" Mia looked up to see a fine white guy. *Damn,* she thought. She was at a loss for words. This man was beautiful.

"Yeah, have a seat," she offered. Never in a million years would Mia have thought she'd be entertaining another man besides Harlem. But here she was with this fine guy all in her face.

"So what's your name, pretty lady?"

"Mia. Yours?"

"Brian."

"Nice to meet you, Brian." They sat and talked for a good hour and, surprisingly, Mia was enjoying herself so much that she was ready to leave with him when he asked her to. Brian was in town on business so they headed to his hotel room at the Marriott. Mia followed him.

"Come on." Brian reached for Mia's hand and suddenly she came to her senses.

"I'm so sorry, Brian. I can't do this." She got back in her car and headed home to her husband. Yeah, he's messed up in the past but that didn't give her the right to do the same. It was time to get things back on track.

When Mia got home Harlem was in the bed asleep." She undressed and got in the bed, scooting close to him.

"Did you get that shit out ya' system?" she was confused.

"Huh?" she asked.

"Don't play games. But just so you know, that white boy is floating in the river somewhere." Mia was shook. She should have known Harlem would find out. They laid in silence until they fell asleep.

Chapter Nineteen
I'm Pregnant

Ryan had been feeling sick lately and had made a doctor's appointment. She told King about the appointment because she had learned her lesson about keeping secrets. She was also scared because of the cancer situation earlier that year. Yeah, she was cancer-free now but they knew there was a chance that it could come back.

"Are you nervous?" King asked Ryan as they waited for the doctor.

"A little. I mean I want another baby, especially since losing Angel, but I don't want to go through the same thing that I did with the last pregnancy." King bent down kissed her forehead.

"It's going to be okay, Ma. God will work it out."

"Okay, Mr. and Mrs. Pierre, I have the results back from your test and you are indeed expecting. I'm going to do an ultrasound so we can see how far you are." The doctor set up the machine and covered Ryan's belly with warm blue gel. After moving the tool around her belly for a minute he spoke again.

"It looks as if you are about sixteen weeks. I actually can see the sex if you guys want to know."

"Yeah, I want to know," King replied.

"This one here is a boy." King was excited to have another boy. This time a Jr.

"Is everything okay with the baby?" King asked.

"As of now, yes. However, I do want you to make an appointment with the oncologist just to follow up." The doctor cleaned Ryan up, gave her a prescription for prenatal vitamins, and headed out.

"Come on, let's get you home, Ma." King helped her off the examination table and they headed out.

"Did you want to stop and grab food?" King asked.

"Nah, but we need to call Marco. I'm going to need him there to make all of our meals so that they are healthier." King called Marco up.

"Marco, what's good man? I'm gonna need you to come back to work if you're available."

King was quiet while Marco spoke.

"Okay, cool man. See you tomorrow." They headed home to share the news with the kids. King was more excited than Ryan because he really wanted the baby they had lost and now they had another chance.

When they got home of course Chasity ran to her dad. He picked her up and they went to the den.

"So Cam, Mommy is having another baby and it's a boy."

"Cool, I'm glad it's a boy because Chasity is too spoiled and we don't need another girl." They laughed.

"Well, it looks like she'll be the only girl. So let's go out and celebrate." They decided to go eat at Fridays, which was one of Ryan's favorite places. That night King held onto Ryan tight as they laid in bed. He said a silent prayer to God for sparing his wife earlier that year. He was truly grateful.

~ ~ ~ ~

Toya had been under the radar but she was back and ready to get King. It was time for Ryan to go. She had waited outside their home until everyone left. Well, at least she thought everyone left. Consuela was still there. Toya headed around back and went in through the back window. She headed upstairs and found the master bedroom. She smiled as she looked around. This was where she was supposed to be. Right in King's bed every night. Yeah her, not Ryan. She laid back on the bed and caught a whiff of King's cologne. That made her panties wet.

"Damn, King, you could fuck me any way you want," she said out loud.

"Who are you and what are you doing in here?" Consuela asked in her thick Spanish accent. Toya jumped up.

She didn't know that anyone was here. She hurried down the stairs and out the door. She had plans on coming back but it would be with King. Some may think that Toya was sick but she just had an infatuation with her older sister's life. Ever since they were younger she'd wanted to be in Ryan's shoes. She headed to the one person that could help her; their dad.

"Toya, what a surprise." She rolled her eyes.

"George." She had never really had a relationship with their father. Her mom was the side chick and she was the hush baby that no one knew about. For that she hated him and his little family. He was there in the home with Ryan but he never did a thing for her. Little did she know Ryan was experiencing hell while she longed for him. Toya had dug up some things in his past and found out what he was in jail for; molesting Ryan.

"So what can I do for you, Toya? I mean, we don't really have the best relationship."

"We don't have one at all but I know we have a common factor." She knew predators don't just stop and if she was right he was looking for Ryan. All she needed for him to do was keep Ryan away from King. After she explained the plan to him, he thought for a minute before agreeing to help her.

"I'm only helping you because it'll benefit me," he had the nerve to say. Toya shook her head at his bluntness.

"Then it's settled. I'll contact you with the details." Toya got up, leaving him sitting at the table. Things were about to get real ugly.

Chapter Twenty
I am the King of Detroit

Four months later....

"Hello, daughter." Ryan instantly stopped in her tracks. She'd never in a million years forget that voice.

"What do you want?" Ryan asked without turning around. She was almost to her car in the parking lot of the mall.

"I just want to talk and, you know, apologize. I want another shot at being your father." Ryan was disgusted.

"No chance in hell." She continued to her car trying to get away from George but being eight months pregnant she wasn't moving fast enough. Before she knew what happened everything went black.

King had been calling Ryan's cell all day but she never answered nor called back. He was worried because she was pregnant. Here it was ten at night and his wife and unborn child were missing. He had called everyone up, including RBM's most loyal members. He knew something wasn't right because Ryan would never disappear like that.

"When was the last time you talked to her?" Harlem asked.

"This morning. She was on her way to the mall to shop. I knew I should have told her to wait." King was so pissed. He was pacing the floor and in an instant he punched the wall.

"Come on man, let's go get some air." Harlem was probably the only person that could calm him down. He took him outside to talk to him.

"Look bro, I know what you going through right now because I was in that position before. I have contacted Ava and we have people on it as we speak. I have also dug up some info on her father like you asked and found out that he was recently released. We also have a trail on Toya. Try and stay calm, bro. We will find her." King heard Harlem, but until Ryan was back home he wasn't about to sit on his ass.

"I hear you bro, but niggas about to see why I'm the King of Detroit. Ain't nobody safe until my wife comes home." King walked away from Harlem. At that point Harlem knew shit was about to get ugly.

"Slow singing and flower bringing," Harlem said to himself.

"Why are you doing this?" Ryan couldn't believe her father had kidnapped her and now had her naked and tied to a bed. He just stared at her never saying anything. He walked over to her and started rubbing on her thighs. Ryan cringed at his touch. *How could someone be so sick?* she thought.

"Ooh and you're pregnant. I know you nice and ripe. I remember when ya' mama was pregnant with you, she had the best pussy ever. I wonder if you taste anything like her." Ryan closed her eyes and prayed that she was saved from this nightmare unharmed. Then she felt a finger slide in her. He was so rough and didn't care that he was sexually assaulting his own daughter.

The tears fell from Ryan's eyes as he moved up to her breasts. He licked each breast sloppily and Ryan felt disgusted. He was just about to penetrate her when the door busted open.

"Back the fuck up, nigga!" Ryan didn't know who that was but she was thankful that they had come when they did.

"Take that nigga to the spot while I call King." Ryan heard King's name. She knew he'd come for her.

"Ayo King, we got her. Alright, bruh, we on the way now." Javon untied Ryan and wrapped her up in a blanket before carrying her to the car. If it wasn't for Toya being sloppy they would have never found her. Apparently she was meeting up with her father about kidnapping Ryan not knowing he had moved ahead of her and snatched Ryan up already. Well, sad to say they both were about to meet their maker. Ryan hadn't even been gone twenty-four hours. People were going to learn to stop underestimating King and his clout.

When Javon pulled up at King's house, King was already waiting outside. He ran to the car to get his wife out. When he saw that she wasn't harmed he thanked God.

"Come on Ma, let's get you in the house." King took her upstairs where he had a bath ran for her. He placed her in the tub and washed her whole body while she cried. King felt bad. What kind of sick person would kidnap and sexually assault their own child? King wouldn't be the one to pull the trigger but George and Toya were as good as dead. There was no way he could let either of them live after what they did to his wife.

An hour later King got the call that George and Toya were no longer breathing. That was all he needed to hear. Now it was time to help his wife with the healing process.

Chapter Twenty-One
The Newest Addition

Ryan was now nine months pregnant and due any day. She was anxious and tired at the same time. She knew that this was their last one. Her body couldn't handle another baby. They had decided to name him after King; KJ for short.

They were at Harlem's house chilling when her water broke.

"Uh King, my water just broke." Everyone got excited. They were ready for the arrival of baby KJ.

"Alright, let's go. Mia, can you drop the kids off to Consuela and then meet us at the hospital?" She agreed and everyone headed out. The made their way to Beaumont Hospital and Ryan was admitted immediately. When they checked her she was seven centimeters dilated.

"Okay mom, it looks as though you'll be ready within the next hour. We're going to put this monitor on you so we can keep track of the contractions as well as the baby's heartbeat," the nurse explained as she hooked Ryan up.

"Are they coming to give her an epidural?" King asked. He saw how much pain Ryan was in and wanted her to be relaxed. He didn't get to see the birth of the twins because of the circumstances but he was here for this one.

"Yes, the doctor has ordered it and the anesthesiologist will in shortly." The nurse headed out. King, Mia, and Helen were in the room with her.

"You okay, Ma?" King asked.

"Yeah, I'm just ready for him to come." King sat next to her and held her hand through every contraction.

Almost two hours later Ryan was fully dilated and ready to push.

"Okay Ryan, when you feel another contraction I want you to push while we count to ten," the nurse told her. King was right there holding one hand and Mia was holding the other.

"One, two, three, four, five, six, seven, eight, nine, ten. Okay, breathe and when you feel another one push again." Ryan repeated that process for all of ten minutes and out came baby KJ. He weighed seven pounds, three ounces, and had a head full of hair. Ryan was exhausted but happy it was over.

"You did good baby." King kissed her on the lips before going over to watch them clean up the baby. He was proud that he got to see his son being born and got to cut the cord.

Mia went to the waiting room to let everyone know that the baby was here. "Hey y'all, he's here and he weighs seven pounds three ounces. King's ass in there all being soft and shit." They laughed.

"Well let us know when we can go back and see them," Yvette said.

"They're cleaning them up now so it shouldn't be too long." They all sat around waiting to go see the new addition to the family.

"Alright, y'all can come see them now," King announced when he came to the waiting room. Everyone followed him to the room where Ryan was already asleep.

"Oh my God, look at him, King!" Kita said. They all took turns holding KJ before they decided to leave so that Ryan could rest. King was happy; his family was complete.

~ ~ ~ ~

"You okay, Ma? You need anything?" Ryan was now home and King was catering to her every need. He was even getting up with the baby at night so that she could rest. He was spending less time in the streets and at the record company. He realized just how much he was missing out on when he was in the streets. He was seriously considering stepping down and letting Rahsaan and Javon run things.

"Nah, I'm good. Thanks baby." Ryan had been going to counseling to get her through the issues with her father, and she was slowly progressing and coming to terms with it. She didn't know why he did it but she had forgiven him; not for him, but so that she could move on with her life.

"Well, I'm going to go put the twins down for their nap and I'll be back." He kissed her lips and headed to their room.

Ryan decided to call Mia. King's birthday was coming up and she wanted to go all out for him. He deserved it. He was back to the man that she had fallen in love with. She was surprised that he had been at home more and not out working. She wasn't complaining, though. She loved him being at home and hoped that it wasn't a temporary thing.

"Hey, Mia girl. What you up to?"

"Girl, just sitting here with Harlem. What's up, Ma?" Mia asked.

"Well, you know King's birthday is coming up and I want to throw him a party. I need ya' help."

"Bitch, you always need my help with something," Mia laughed.

"Shut up fool, and just meet me tomorrow for lunch so we can discuss the plans."

"Okay, cool. See ya' tomorrow." Ryan hung up and headed to the shower.

Chapter Twenty-Two
Party Like a Rock Star

It was the night of King's birthday party and he had no clue. He just thought he was chilling with his brother and his crew. Ryan had said she didn't want to hang out because she was too tired so he let her be. She insisted that he go out and celebrate so he did.

"So where we headed?" King asked.

"To Club Skyy to get fucked up," Harlem replied. When they pulled up it was mad crowded. King thought it was rather odd for a Thursday night but he shrugged it off. When they walked in everybody yelled "Surprise!" All of RBM was there, even some from out of town and Ryan was even there with the biggest smile on her face. King walked right to her and grabbed her by the waist. "Thanks, Ma." He kissed her for what seemed like an eternity.

"Get a room. We're here to party!" Kita shouted.

"Hater," Ryan replied.

"Come on y'all, we got a section up here." Harlem led the way to VIP. Everybody was on the other side of the rope yelling to King. It was either "Happy birthday" or "Can I go home with you?" Ryan laughed at the thirsty chicks that wanted him. She wasn't worried because she had him.

"Let me get a few bottles of Ace of Spades, an Amaretto Sour for my wife, and a bottle of Remy," King ordered. Beyoncé's "Dance For You" came on and King wanted a dance.

"Can I get a lap dance, Ma?" Ryan smiled and then led him to a private area. She didn't want to put on a show for the whole club. She grabbed a chair, told King to sit, and started dancing provocatively. King was mesmerized as if it was his first time seeing her dance. She bent over and touched her toes while shaking her ass in his face. He pulled out a knot of money and started putting in her waistband. She turned around and jiggled her breasts in his face. He pulled her close and kissed her but she moved away too quick. There was another chair across from his so she sat down and then opened her legs to give him a pussy shot. King was gone at that point. He got up and pulled her to the corner. He wanted some pussy. He lifted her up on the wall and pulled his dick out. He had her skirt up just enough to give him access. He pushed his dick in her and she cried out in pleasure. Sex with King was always good.

"Damn Ma, ya' shit leaking." As King thrust in and out of her he professed his love for her.

"Damn, King! Ooh….shit….that's…um…my spot. Oh shit!" Ryan hit her first orgasm. But King wasn't done with her. He wanted her to cum at least once more. He knew her spot and he hit once again.

"Fuck, King!" She bit his shoulder.

"Damn, Ma!" King shot his seeds all in her. "Damn, that shit was good. Come on, let's go clean you up." They headed to the bathroom before going back to VIP.

"Where y'all freaks go?" Kita joked.

"Man, get out of their business," Markie spoke up. Kita rolled her eyes.

"Come on, let's dance." Mia grabbed Harlem. He wasn't really a dancer but if Mia wanted it, she got it. They partied and danced until three in the morning. King enjoyed his birthday and family. He really appreciated Ryan and knew that he had a down as chick. His sister Ava wasn't able to make it but she sent his gift, which was an Audemars Piguet watch. Ryan cashed out and got him a Bentley Continental GT. He liked that gift the most. Harlem and Mia bought him some new Cartier frames and Tez, Vette, Markie, and Kita got him an all-expense-paid trip to the Bahamas. Once they left the club King took Ryan home to bang her back out. It was something about a bad bitch.

~ ~ ~ ~

"Thanks, Ma." Ryan smiled.

"It's cool, bae. I wanted your b-day to be the bomb."

"Nah, not just for the birthday, but for being you. You hold a nigga down even when I act an ass. You a bad bitch, no disrespect intended. We have been through a lot and you still rocking with a nigga. You had my seeds and you're the best damn mom." Ryan kissed King.

"Boy, you know I got ya' back 'til the world blow. Ain't no bitch got shit on me. That's why you put a ring on it," she joked.

"Hell yeah. I had to cuff that ass. If I didn't then some busta' ass nigga would have. But nah Ma, seriously, I love you." King couldn't believe he was doing what he was about to do.

"Ma, I'm out the game. A nigga got what he need right here at home. I'm letting Rahsaan and Javon handle all that shit. The record company is still mine but they're running it. I want to be here for you and my kids. And I want to adopt Cam. I mean, I know he's mine regardless but I wanna make it official." Ryan had tears in her eyes. This was all she wanted. Not to change King but for him to realize there was more to life than the dope game. And he finally realized it before it was too late.

"Baby you don't know how much that means to me. Every day I worry about something happening to you."

"Well, I'm done, Ma and I'm here with you. I love you."

"I love you too, King."

Epilogue
No Greater Love

Everything that Ryan and King had been through taught them a lesson. They had obstacles in their relationship but through it all they survived. Their relationship had come full circle.

At the end of the day Ryan and King shared a bond that was unbreakable. Even those times when they were apart the bond was still there. They showed what for better or worse really meant. Ryan proved that she was his Bonnie and he was her Clyde. King learned how to love Ryan and not be so quick to react. His biggest issue was trust because he had never been in love before Ryan. He had brought the issues of his past relationships into their relationship. Had they never worked past that, they would have been doomed from the beginning. But things always have a way of working out for the good.

King had officially adopted Cameron. He was already his son but it was official now; their family was complete. Ryan let go of what her dad did. She knew to get past her demons she had to. Toya got what she was asking for. King didn't feel sorry at all. She wanted Ryan's life and was willing to do whatever to get it. What she failed to realize is you can't make a person love you. King never told Ryan about Toya being her sister. He didn't feel she needed to know. That was another issue that would have caused her hurt. King had found his soul mate; even if it took him a minute to realize it.

Harlem and Mia, as usual, were good. They were known as the Jay-Z and Beyoncé of the 'hood. They had that 'hood love that went back to their teenage years and that couldn't be broken. It had been two years and Ryan's cancer has yet to return. Thank God for the small blessings.

THE END

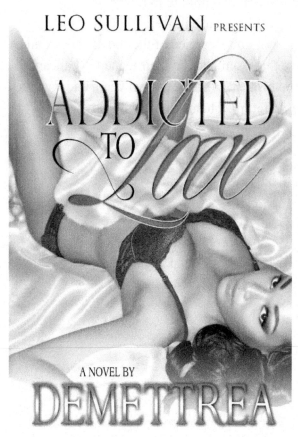

Check out more books by Demettrea

Coming soon…..

Coming

June 12th......
Coming Soon......

Coming soon…..

Coming Soon….

CPSIA information can be obtained
at www.ICGtesting.com
Printed in the USA
LVOW04s0039310116

473031LV00011B/53/P